P9-CDK-297

Secrets of the Charles

By

Susan Boyd

© 2011 Susan Boyd
All Rights Reserved.

No part of this publication may be reproduced, stored in a retrieval system, or
transmitted, in any form or by any means, electronic, mechanical, photocopying,
recording, or otherwise, without the written permission of the author.

First published by Dog Ear Publishing
4010 W. 86th Street, Ste H
Indianapolis, IN 46268
www.dogearpublishing.net

ISBN: 978-145750-267-5

This book is printed on acid-free paper.

This book is a work of fiction. Places, events, and situations in this book are
purely fictional and any resemblance to actual persons, living or dead, is coinci-
dental.

Printed in the United States of America

This book is dedicated to Arthur L. Boyd
(Larry) – my husband and best friend.
I bless the day I picked you up
at your daughter's wedding.

APPRECIATION

My thanks go out to many people for their help and encouragement during the writing of this book.

Cousins Elaine Allen and Jeanne Ireland for giving me honest appraisals of the first draft, as well as historical background of Boston and life in the fifties and sixties.

Officer Joe Zanoli, Boston Police Department, for his insight into the police department's organization and procedures.

Mary Lois Sanders for her excellent editing skills.

Members of the Creative Writers Group in The Villages, Florida for their constructive critiques and encouragement.

Friends and family members who read early drafts of the book. I took your comments to heart in polishing the final version.

Yellow tape held taut across Jack and his two high school buddies, as their necks craned, searching the scene on the Charles River. Their bikes were strewn under a nearby tree. Red police car lights strobed against the crisp fall afternoon air, mesmerizing the crowd.

The police diver gently placed the body in the net.

"Doesn't look like a jumper," the diver muttered to himself. "Not thrown in either."

Her hair formed a halo around a pretty face not yet bloated from the river's murky water. Her flowered dress twisted tightly around her shapely body. Ends of the scarf around her neck floated like angel's wings. She hadn't rested in her watery grave for long. The diver gave a thumbs-up to the crew, and her body floated past him to the river's bank.

Jack and his friends altered their positions for a better view when the officers shifted, opening a window to the woman's face.

Suddenly, a guttural, animal wail pierced the air. Jack collapsed into the arms of his friends.

From the bridge, a man watched – fedora jauntily tipped, sunglasses shielding out the sun, masking any expression. He exchanged glances with a young police officer, and then nodded. The man's stare turned from the dead woman to Jack.

"I'm so sorry," he muttered before turning his back on the scene.

"Incoming!" One simple word struck terror in combatants.

"Take cover!" Jack shouted, as he turned for his foxhole. An instinct, borne of training and self-preservation, catapulted him. In the few steps to his destination, time warped, slowly moving forward, like viewing the scene in individual frames of a film reel.

A soldier's back arched. His body convulsed as he fell forward, face engulfed by the soft muck of the rain-soaked earth.

A bullet pierced another soldier's head – crimson ribbons and spots suspended in the air as the round traveled through his skull.

Time accelerated, regaining its normalcy. Jack tucked and rolled into the pit of his foxhole, mud spraying. He hugged his knees, head down. The ground spit chunks, synchronized with the whizz and crack of bullets punctuating the air.

Then, silence.

Slowly, Jack uncoiled from the fetal position, squatting in the hole. He slung the M-16 over his shoulder, positioned it – left hand on the forward grip, stock firmly imbedded against his shoulder, right finger on the trigger. His eyes scanned the field. Only two dead. The corporal in the next foxhole pantomimed the location of the enemy. Jack nodded.

A primordial instinct captured Jack's brain, switching from flight to fight. He bellowed as his finger worked the trigger in short bursts. Around him, puffs of smoke floated in the air, the familiar stench of cordite assaulted his nostrils. His unit was fighting back.

Jack felt the well-placed punch to his solar plexus. One more pull on the trigger. One more step. Knees buckling, he landed on the ground with a thud, the ooze of the earth barely breaking his fall. Pain seared in his gut. He wiped his hand across the gaping hole, feeling the heat of the sticky wetness. Pulling his hand away, he studied the scarlet liquid rivers flowing down his wrist. A humming sound contorted the noise of the battle.

"Medic! Lieutenant's down!" someone shouted. Hovering faces blurred, voices echoed. Jack shivered.

"Jack. Jack. Stay with me," the medic yelled. Then, turning to someone, "All I can do for now."

Jack felt the warmth enter his vein, as he succumbed to the darkness.

Memories swirled in Jack's head. Footballs spiraling from his hand. Harmonious voices warbling in song. Holiday lights. Birthday candles. Memories of Kate smiling, laughing, singing. A sudden shift to dark thoughts. Kate crying.

He left her a parting gift, in case he didn't return. Not to cause her pain – only to give back her love. She never deserted him. He pushed her away. Had to.

Then, turmoil. The nightmarish vision of his mother lying by the river. His father and siblings crying. Grey, distorted images faded as his mother reappeared. Beautiful, smiling. He reached for her hand. She sang to him, guided him.

"Kate."

His last word before entering the light.

Half-way across the world, Kate wept.

PART ONE

LILITH

CHAPTER 1

"Morning, Lilith. Hubby gone? Kids gone? Coffee on?" Kate asked in rapid succession, shuffling across the kitchen in her ratty, purple slippers. I swear she's been wearing those same slippers since the seventies – or at least replicas. Kate's my mother. From my earliest memories, she insisted I call her by her first name. I, on the other hand, insisted my children refer to me by the more traditional title.

"Alexa's still upstairs getting dressed," I responded. "Late night?"

"Don't ask," Kate said, joining me at the table with her coffee in hand. Subject closed. When she moved in with us five years ago, we mutually adopted a "don't ask, don't tell" policy. For the six months each year she resided in the renovated space above our garage, she hoarded her privacy like a child with Halloween candy. Although connected to the house on the second floor, her suite also had its own outside entrance. When she moved in, I expected her help with raising my children. She ended up being their favorite entertainer.

Alexa's entrance was preceded by the tapping of her heels in the hallway. I turned, mug in hand, ready to greet her to the day. I stopped short.

"Alexandra Elizabeth Callahan, you are NOT wearing that outfit to a job interview," I yelled.

Turning to her grandmother, Alexa's face feigned angelic pleading. She twirled, showing off her clothes.

"What do you think, Nana Kate?"

"Sorry, kiddo. I'm with your mother on this one. A pink, polka-dotted mini-dress that barely covers your hoo-hah, fishnet stockings, and white patten leather boots are more suited for school than work."

"Kate," I said, voice strained with frustration, "you're not really helping."

"Wait a minute," Kate paused, looking at Alexa. "Where did you get that outfit?"

"I found it in one of your old wardrobes in the attic. I thought it looked quite – how do you say it – groovy."

"Thought it looked familiar. I believe I wore it to The Who concert."

"What's a Who?" Alexa asked.

"Oh, The Who was a band in the 60's," Kate said, eyes glazing over as she propped her chin in her hands. "What a great memory that one is. I went with Tommy. No, Bobby. Um, no, Pete. Oh heck, I can't remember. There were just too many guys in those days." Still attractive in her late sixties, Kate was a man-magnet. Her petite, shapely frame, dark naturally-curly hair, and almond shaped eyes turned heads wherever she went.

"We're getting off topic here," I said. "Now Alexa, go upstairs and change into that nice suit I bought you."

Breathing a heavy, dramatic sigh, Alexa turned and clomped out of the kitchen. I heard the fading echo of her boots as she ascended the stairs, walked down the hall, and slammed into her bedroom.

Kate looked wistfully at the doorway vacated by Alexa's dramatic exit.

"You know, she looks better in that outfit than I ever did. I think it's her height. She gets that from Bill. But her legs. Now, she gets those from me … and you."

Although I was considered on the tall side for a woman – five-six – Alexa topped my height by the same inches I topped Kate – three.

"Speaking of Bill," I said, trying to jog Kate back from her daydreams, "he pulled some strings to get her that interview with the police department."

"Oh, face it, Lilith. Bill's a prominent attorney in this town. He didn't have to pull too hard on any strings. Plus, she's majoring in criminal justice. She's the perfect candidate for the internship. You really should go easier on her. Alexa's a good kid, with brains to boot. They'll be lucky to have her for the summer."

"I know she's a good kid," I conceded. "But sometimes it just seems like it's an uphill battle with her. Like that time in high school. She went through that phase when she thought she was a witch."

"Wiccan, not witch," Kate corrected.

"You're splitting hairs. I know she didn't try to fly around on a broom or cast evil spells. Although, I did regularly check her room for voodoo dolls and eye of newt."

"Oh, Lilith. You never did understand her fascination with Wicca. So instead, she used to come to me to talk about it. It really wasn't harmful. She was just searching for something to believe in not so traditionally dominated by men and her parents. It's about being concerned with the balance of nature. It has nothing to do with trying to manipulate, control or harm people."

"So, is this better?" Alexa asked, re-entering the kitchen in the conservative navy blue suit I'd bought her several days earlier. Hoop earrings the size of bracelets dangled from her ears, matching the over-sized lapel pin angled from her left shoulder. Not the style of jewelry I'd choose, but with her height she carried it off.

"Much better," I said. "You look so professional now."

"Well then, I'll just go to the closet and get my broom out so I won't be late for the interview." Alexa winked at Kate.

"Oh, and just so you guys get it straight," Alexa continued, "I'm still Wiccan. Nana Kate has it basically right. But there's one belief I still try to follow. It's called the Law of Return."

"What's that, honey?" Kate asked.

"It says all the good a person does to another returns three-fold in this life, and harm is also returned three-fold. So, there's strength in threes. See you later."

Alexa smiled widely, turned – her long, blonde hair whipping to the side before gently settling in its natural curls down her back – and left.

"She is a pistol," Kate said, chuckling.

As I walked over to the sink, her chuckle turned into a giggle before erupting into a full laugh. I mentally slapped my forehead.

"You put her up to that outfit, didn't you?" I asked.

"You are just too easy," Kate replied through snorts of laughter.

"Am not." I caught my reflection in the window, smiling back at me. Yeah, I was easy.

CHAPTER 2

"Hi hon," Bill said as he wrapped one arm around my waist, and then leaned in for a kiss.

It was our daily ritual. I got butterflies when I heard the garage door open at the end of each day. After twenty-two years of marriage, he still rocked my boat.

We met in college. I was a sophomore – major in journalism, minor in sociology – and he was in his first year of law school. One Wednesday night – hump day – I sat at a table with a couple of friends at our usual watering hole off campus. Demurely sipping some pink froo-froo drink, I suddenly had the sensation someone was looking at me. Trying to be coy, I slowly turned and locked eyes with the most beautiful smile I had ever seen – from the amused glint in his crinkled eyes to the broad, toothy smile, showing off dimples. I smiled in return.

Weaving through the crowd around the bar, he approached, his head clearly visible above most other patrons. I started to get up to meet him face-to-face, but he gently put his hand on my shoulder and whispered in my ear.

"Don't try to stand up," he whispered. "Your skirt is caught in the chair. If you stand up, you may rip it. By the way … nice ass."

I was horrified. How was I going to get dislodged without creating a scene, or displaying more derriere? Then this man flirting with me nonchalantly moved behind me to block the view. I half-turned, struggling with my skirt, yanking it back and forth to free the caught material. As the skirt loosened the final bit from the chair rung, my hands flew upward, smacking him in the balls. His smile turned to a slight grimace, as he gently sat in the chair next to me.

"Oh my god, I'm so sorry! Are-are you okay?" I stuttered. "Can I get you anything? Another drink? Some aspirin? Some ice? A bandage? Should I go get help from one of your buddies?"

"No, no, don't do that. I'll be fine. Thank goodness you punch like a girl." The smile returned, a bit less broad than from across the room.

"By the way," he said, extending his hand, "my name is Bill. I figure since I've seen your ass and you've hit me in the gonads, we should be formally introduced."

"I'm Lilly," I said, shaking his hand.

From that first meeting, we were inseparable. Everyone commented we looked like Barbie and Ken dolls. Both blondes, my hair was light golden, and his a sandy, ash shade. We got married the summer after our graduations. Deciding to make an independent start, we moved to DC, and into a small apartment in northern Virginia. Bill got a job with a law firm representing the alcohol industry. I started as a cub reporter in a suburban newspaper, assigned to obits.

A year later, I was pregnant. As the morning sickness subsided, I realized I was homesick. I missed New England. I wanted my children raised with their aunts and uncles and cousins and grandparents, within a short commute. Bill easily agreed. His earlier fascination with DC had worn thin. He landed a job with a firm in Boston, and we headed north.

Two children and twenty years later, Bill was a senior partner in the law firm. When the children started school, I went back to work as an investigative reporter. After ten years of chasing the gore, I decided to start free-lancing instead, writing a variety of articles for newspapers and magazines. We live in our third house since returning to the Boston area – my dream house. A large colonial, built in the early nineteen-hundreds, renovated with all the modern conveniences.

"What smells so good? Besides you, that is," Bill said, nuzzling my neck.

"I'm fixing Alexa's favorite dish, chicken paprikash."

"Is it a special occasion?"

"She had that job interview today, with the police department. I figure I should make her feel special whether she got the job, or not."

"That's nice," Bill said, then paused listening to sounds from the den. "I hear Johnny's home. What's he's playing now?" Johnny was our sixteen-year-old son.

"They've been working on a medley of Beatles' songs. Kate's been trying to get him interested in rock music. I guess it's better than rap. I try tuning it out so I don't end up the day with a headache. Some days I wish Kate had never bought him that stupid toy piano on his first birthday."

"But remember how quickly he progressed once he started taking lessons? I do believe the kid has talent. Must get it from your side of the family. I'm pretty much tone deaf."

"Yeah," I sighed. "And Kate does enjoy being his muse. She switches his tunes from Elvis hits to Motown, to folk music, to Beatles. It's like she morphs between her rock 'n roll, beatnik and hippie days. I think she's now stuck as a hippie."

"At least they'll be done with their jam session by dinner time," Bill said, pouring himself a scotch and water. "Want some wine?"

"Sure. Dinner's about done. It can simmer until Alexa gets home with her news." I headed to my favorite kitchen stool at the center island. Although our spacious kitchen included a round table we used for breakfast, I preferred to prop myself on a stool during pre-supper cocktail time.

"Speaking of Alexa," Bill said, settling onto a stool next to me, "don't you think it's about time you told her about her grandfather's family?"

"I really dread that discussion," I groaned. "Both of the kids already know their grandfather died in Vietnam. Kate told them that much years ago. I guess Alexa's old enough to know the rest. I'm just not sure Johnny is though."

"How old were you when Kate told you?"

"Eighteen. But God, it was so traumatic." I shuddered at the memory. In one fell blow, Kate not only told me about artificial insemination, but also the ugliness of my grandmother's death. Her murder was never solved. Strangled and dumped in the Charles River. The big family mystery.

Thoughts of that conversation brought on a headache and memories of a recurring nightmare from my teens and early twenties. I was floating over a scene, just a casual observer. A woman glided along murky water on her back. She looked like an angel. Eyes closed, limbs catching the motion of the waves. Somehow in my dream, I realized she was dead. Then, she was on dry land. Flashes of red strobed in the background. People

9

gathered around her. A figure floated toward her. I couldn't tell whether it was male or female. It lifted something over its head. Suddenly, the dead woman's eyes popped open and she looked directly at me, trying to say something. As I stared into her eyes, reflecting the brilliance of the blue sky, I became her. It was me who floated, then lay on the hard ground. Three men stood by my side, holding onto a red scarf. Just before a stone face, held by the floating figure, crashed into my head, I awoke, drenched.

I shook my head to erase the flashback.

CHAPTER **3**

"So, tell all. How did the interview go?" Kate asked as Alexa entered the kitchen.

"It was fine. I got the job. They introduced me around a bit."

"Well, congratulations, honey," Kate said, giving Alexa a hug. "When do you start? What will you be doing?"

"Kate, let's wait until we sit down for dinner before starting the interrogation," I said, heading into the dining room with the entree.

"Look, honey," Kate said, "your mom fixed your favorite meal."

"And I made dessert – my famous chocolate-chip granola cookies," Johnny added, grinning widely.

"Thanks, Mom. It's great, as always," Alexa said between bites.

Watching Kate as she tapped her fork on the plate after every bite, I knew she was itching to find out more about the interview, but refrained herself, waiting for Alexa. Halfway through the meal, she stared doe-eyed at Alexa, willing her to start talking. I stifled a giggle. It was a ploy Kate used whenever she wanted someone to give her information. She stared and wriggled her leg up and down. I always thought she was keeping time to some tune in her head. Or perhaps a private mantra. Finally Alexa relented.

"I was interviewed by the chief and a couple of officers. They asked me about the courses I'm taking, and what my plans are after I earn my degree. Then they had a couple of hypothetical questions to test my ethics. At the end of the interview, they asked if I had a preference on where to spend my internship."

"What were the hypotheticals?" I asked, curious how they could figure out someone's ethics through an interview.

"They had to do with taking bribes. Like what if someone in lockup hinted he could get me a special price on a car if I turned around while a visitor gives him something. As if. Then, they asked what I'd do if I found out another officer had agreed to the offer. Shit. It was rather lame, actually."

"You didn't answer the questions that way, did you?" I asked, knowing Alexa was prone to sarcasm.

"No, Mom. I was as polite and professional as my suit. Anyway, after the interview, once they told me I had the internship, one of the officers took me to a squad room and introduced me to some of the guys."

"So, when do you start?" Kate restarted her interrogation. "What will you be doing? What are they like there? Did they issue you a uniform?"

"Or a gun?" Johnny added.

"I start on Monday, helping the cops with their paperwork. I guess there are lots of forms they have to fill out. They said I'll also be helping out with some cold cases. No uniform. No gun. After I get familiar with everything, they'll let me ride along with them from time to time."

"You won't be in any danger during the ride-alongs, will you?" I asked.

"They won't put her in harm's way," Bill said, patting my leg. "I'm sure if something happens, she'll be told to stay in the car."

"Did you meet anyone interesting?" Kate asked.

"I was introduced to two of the detectives who work cold cases. One was really cute. And I think he's single. The other one was older, fatter, and surly."

"So, tell us more," Kate said. "Especially about the cute one." Resting her face in her hand, she turned expectantly to Alexa. Again, the doe-eyed stare.

"His name is Ryan Brady. He's about six feet tall, probably in his mid-to-late twenties, dark hair, and hazel eyes. And long, thick eyelashes. He has one of those natural-looking perpetual tans. And a slight cleft in his chin. On the other hand, his partner is about five-nine, balding, with a pot belly. His name is Frank Scapini."

"Well, I think Ryan sounds yummy," Kate said. "Maybe I'll come visit you and take you to lunch one day. Then, I can check him out."

"Kate, please," I shouted. "She's there to work, not pick up men."

"Oh hell, Mom," Alexa said. "Chill out. Nana Kate's just kidding around. Besides, he's much too young for her. Unless he's into mature women. I don't know. Maybe I'll ask him."

I threw my hands up in resignation. Once again, I let them get to me. When would I learn not to take their bait?

CHAPTER **4**

"I swear, I don't know how the girl survives in college," I mumbled, picking up clothes strewn around her room. Alexa's internship was in its second week, and I swore she hadn't done laundry during that time. The chore reminded me of her high school years, and I grinned. Turn them right-side out. Check the pockets.

"What's this?" I asked myself. I held a three-inch white-papered object by my fingertips. A joint.

"Son-of-a-BITCH," I shouted. I thought she was past her experimentation phase. But then, I'd thought she was over her witch phase, too. How could she be doing drugs while working for the police? I felt the flush start at my neck, working its way to the top of my head, as I fought back tears of frustration. Pacing around the room, my heart pounded. I grabbed the laundry basket and stomped down the stairs to the basement.

I had to keep busy, stay calm. I retreated back upstairs to the office and booted up the computer. I was working on several stories. I couldn't concentrate on the one about a child molester. I opened the document on the newest diet craze. Some ditz swore that if you ate only eggs, grapes and carrots for a week you'd lose five to ten pounds. No shit. But I had to remain objective in my reporting. I finished the piece in a couple of hours, and then emailed it to the publisher. The small sense of accomplishment tamed my anger.

"Hi, hon." Bill's usual greeting and kiss did little to abate my mood.

"What's wrong?" he asked. He could always tell when I was troubled. I started to say, "Nothing," but knew he would prod until I spilled my guts. I told him about my find.

"Maybe there's a reasonable explanation," Bill said. "Please give her a chance to tell us."

"Well, I'm not holding dinner for her," I said, stomping out of the kitchen with the dishes. "Kate. Johnny. Dinner's ready," I shouted.

"Aren't we waiting for Alexa?" Kate asked as she took her seat.

"Nope." My one-word reply spoke volumes. Silence prevailed at the table.

Alexa strolled in, sat down, eyes wandering around at each of us.

"What's up?" she asked.

"We'll talk about it after dinner," I replied. More silence. Sensing he was off the hook, Johnny excused himself before dessert was served. Kate cleared the table. I glared at Alexa.

"Look what I found in your jeans pocket," I said, pulling the joint out of my shirt pocket.

"What? Are you spying on me now? I'm in college, damn it. Almost twenty. Not some high school kid you can monitor twenty-four, seven."

"Do NOT turn this around."

"What's that?" Kate asked, returning to the dining room. She examined the joint as I held onto it. "Uh, oh," was her only comment.

"Okay, Mom. What do you want to know?"

"Are you doing drugs again? You're working for the police, for Pete's sake."

"Someone gave it to me at a party last weekend. I just stuck it in my pocket. I'm not doing drugs."

"So, why did you take it then?" Bill asked, taking over the interrogation.

"I don't know, Dad. I guess I thought I'd keep it in case I got over-stressed at some point."

"Well, you'll just have to cope without it now," I announced.

"I'll hold onto it, if you want," Kate offered.

"No," we all replied in unison. Kate shrugged, as I pocketed the joint. I could think of nothing else to say, retreating to the kitchen.

"How about we go out on the porch?" Kate said to Alexa.

I heard the front screen door close. Bill followed me into the kitchen.

"Honey, we have to trust her," he said. "She's doing well in school. She's enjoying her summer job – even talking about joining the force after college. I don't think she'll jeopardize it all by doing something stupid. Maybe you should join them out on the porch. I'll finish up here." He wrapped his arms around me, kissing the top of my head.

Standing inside the screen door, I tried to calm myself. I listened to their conversation as I leaned against the door frame.

"You're not going to lecture me, are you, Nana Kate?"

"Oh, I'm not the one to lecture you," Kate said, chuckling. "After all, I have no room to talk." She hesitated before continuing.

"I know you and your mother don't always see eye-to-eye, but she loves you dearly and worries about you."

"But sometimes she treats me like an adolescent," Alexa replied. "It's just so frustrating. I honestly don't know what I was going to do with the joint when I took it. Actually, I had forgotten about it until just now."

"You're lucky to have a mother who cares so much. She really is a better mother to you than I was to her. I don't know how she turned out the way she did. I know when I named her, I had visions of her being much different."

"What do you mean?" Alexa asked.

"Haven't you ever heard the story about the name Lilith?"

"Uh, no. I didn't know there was story to be told."

"Well, one semester when I was in college," Kate began, "I took a course in mythology. I was also taking a philosophy course at the same time. Both had female professors, which made for interesting discussions. Anyway, we studied the myth of Lilith, and I brought it up for discussion in the philosophy class for a different perspective. It was all quite lively." Kate paused. "According to the legend, Lilith was Adam's first wife."

"You mean as in Adam and Eve?"

"The one and only. Anywho, God created Adam and Lilith from the same material, so they were equals. When Lilith refused to lie beneath Adam, he got pissed. She got even more pissed and left him. She retreated to her home by the Red Sea, and started having fun with the bad boys. Adam whined to God, saying he didn't want to go back to sleeping with animals. So, God created Eve out of Adam's rib, thus making her subservient to him.

"The myth goes on to blame Lilith and the daughters of Lilith for the infidelities of men through the ages. She was a temptress. Of course, men weren't to blame for straying from their wives. It was all Lilith's fault."

I could almost hear Kate's eyes rolling. Standing by the door, I recalled when Kate told me about my namesake. I was fourteen years old. I remember screaming at her, "You named me for a she-devil?" From that moment, I insisted everyone call me Lilly. But Kate never did. I never heard the rest of her explanation, until now.

"So, you named mom after a temptress?" Alexa asked.

"That's not the point, honey. Lilith was the first strong woman created. She was equal to men, not subservient to them. I hoped your mother would somehow inherit that strength and always be independent-minded."

"Well, she's not exactly a wimp."

"Yeah, but she ended up being more of a fluffy girl than I envisioned. After all, she was a cheerleader in high school. But I guess that was my mother's influence. All in all though, she turned out pretty well."

Hearing my mother tell this story diffused the anger at my daughter. I knew eventually I would have to reveal other family mysteries to her.

CHAPTER 5

"I had such a great day today," Alexa exclaimed as she sat down for dinner a week after the joint escapade.

"What, did Ryan ask you out?" Kate asked.

"No. Not yet anyway. First, a couple of detectives took me out on a ride-along." Alexa was unusually animated – eyes sparkling, talking fast, hands moving all over the place.

My heart skipped a beat.

"They were doing an interview on a case about some old murder," Alexa continued, "and they had me take notes. We went to Revere to talk to a store clerk in this really grubby little market. The guy was this skinny, slimy little character, who spoke broken English. The plan was all three of us would watch his body language while he was talking to see if we could pick up clues to when he was lying. The course I took in Kinesics last semester really came in handy."

"What's kinesics?" Kate asked.

"The study of non-verbal communication, also known as body language. In fact, some studies show as much as ninety-three percent of communication is non-verbal. But it's really only about seventy percent."

"So, when I flip someone the bird it's considered non-verbal communication?" Kate asked, waving her extended middle finger.

"Well, yes," Alexa chuckled. "But it's more than hand gestures. You have to look at facial expressions, how someone holds their body, and movement of the arms and legs."

"So how did this work during your interview?" I asked.

"Well, they were doing the good cop, bad cop thing. One calmly asking questions, while the other was stomping around the store. They were trying to keep him off guard. Whenever I noticed a telltale movement, I'd jot it down in the notes. Now and then, the good cop would look over at my notes."

"What kind of telltale sign?" I asked.

"Like this one time, when he was asked about the robbery, the guy's eyes shifted to the left while he was answering. Since he was right-handed, that showed he was making up the answer. If he had been recalling what actually happened, he would have looked to the right. Anyway, after about a half hour of this nonsense, the good cop looked at the guy and said, 'We know you faked the robbery and gave the money to Maria to hold for you.' Maria is the dead woman. Then they cuffed him and put him in the car."

"You rode in the same car as some murderer?" I was trying to remain calm.

"I got in the front seat and the bad cop sat with him in the back. Don't worry, Mom, I was safe."

"So, what happened to the guy?" Bill asked.

"After they Mirandized him, they continued the interview back at the station. I watched from behind the mirror. It took no time for them to get the guy to admit he killed Maria when she threatened to tell his boss about the money. It was so cool."

"Well, that must have been exciting," Kate said, pausing ever so briefly. "So, what else happened today?"

Alexa looked at Kate, blinking rapidly and shook her head. It always took a beat or two to catch up with Kate's sudden changes in the topic of conversation.

"Well, other than getting to use, in a real-life situation, something I studied, I heard back from my professor at college. I had asked him about earning credits for the work I'm doing this summer. He called the lieutenant and they came up with a plan. I can get three whole credits if I do research on a cold case and write a paper. Isn't that awesome?"

"Oh honey, how cool," Kate replied. "Have you picked one out yet?"

"Well, I talked to Frank and Ryan about it. They suggested several cases they were working on. But I wanted something that had not been worked yet. Wouldn't be fair if they already half solved it. Kinda like cheating. But there are just so many possibilities. How can I choose? I want a really old case. Something everyone gave up on."

Kate's fork clattered to her plate, drawing everyone's attention. She looked down at her hands, sighed, and then looked up at Alexa.

"I have a case for you," Kate said.

"No-o-o," I half screamed, half moaned.

"It's time she knew," Kate said, giving me a forlorn look. "It's time we all knew everything."

Bill and I froze, turned to each other, then to Kate.

"A woman named Julia O'Shea was murdered in 1958," Kate said, voice cracking. Her eyes dropped back to her lap.

"I don't understand," Alexa said, looking at Bill and me. "Did you guys know this woman? How could you? You weren't even born yet. In fact, Nana Kate was younger than me."

"I was seventeen," Kate whispered.

"Wait a minute," Alexa said, pursing her lips, eyes rolling to the ceiling. "O'Shea ... O'Shea." She paused. "Isn't that the last name of my grandfather?" Alexa looked expectantly around the table.

"Yes, dear," Kate sighed, looking up, straightening her shoulders. "Julia O'Shea was your great grandmother."

PART TWO

KATE

Reflecting on Julia's death brought a torrent of memories, from first meeting Jack in our freshman year of high school, to Lilith's unconventional birth ten years later. It was a turbulent time of rivals, romance, repression and ... well ... death. It all started on the first day of ninth grade.

Let's see – 340, 341, 342, here it is – 343. My locker.

Ignoring other students struggling with the combinations on adjacent lockers, I concentrated on my lock's dial.

"I think they put these things on our lockers just to make us suffer, don't you?" asked an unknown voice.

I peeked around the metal door to answer, and looked right into the face of the head cheerleader from junior high. Large, vacant, blue eyes. Bleached blonde hair, pulled back in a pony-tail and wrapped in a scarf matching her outfit. What did I do to the gods to deserve this?

"I'm Missy Jamison," she squeaked. "Isn't it just so nifty to be in high school?"

"Hi, I'm Kate Gallagher," I replied. Before I could offer to help her with the high-level mechanics of opening a lock, I was startled by shrieking coming from someplace down the hall.

"Misseeee," echoed through the corridor. Suddenly, I was surrounded by perky cheerleaders, ponytails, short bobbed dos and little boobs bouncing everywhere. I stepped aside, search-ing my locker for my History book.

"We missed you so-o-o much this summer," one of the perky bunch squealed. "How was the Cape?"

"It was a kick. Mostly just mom and me. Dad kept going back to the city on business. Mom wasn't too happy about that. But who cares? Kept her off my back."

"Have you seen Jack yet?" another of her entourage asked. "He worked for his dad's construction company over the sum-mer, and his muscles are just the most. You'll swoon when you see him."

"No, I haven't seen him yet," Missy said, lips pursed in a pout. "And I can't wait for him to get a peep at my tan. He'll come crawling back to me this fast." Missy snapped her fingers. Ponytails and curls bobbed in agreement.

Everyone from junior high knew Jack O'Shea, the star quarterback, plus one of the top students. He and Missy went steady in the eighth grade, voted king and queen of some big dance. I didn't pay much attention to the goings on of their crowd, so I was somewhat clueless about the budding romance. From Missy's comment, I surmised Jack split with her at some point. Didn't know why. Didn't care.

"Lookie," the squealer whispered. "There he is. And his locker's only," she hesitated counting the lockers, "nine away from yours, Missy." She must have been the smart one of the group – she could count.

Just then, the bell announcing first period rang. Lockers slammed as students scampered around the hallway to the classrooms. The first day was a test-run for the students – a half day. Each class only lasted fifteen minutes. The bell rang, giving students 10 minutes for the race to the next room on their schedules. No lunch period.

Missy's menagerie locked arms, skipped down the hallway chanting an apparently new cheer, "We're so fine, most divine, we're the class of fifty-nine."

I groaned.

Seated alphabetically in each class, I always ended up in a middle spot. Last period – Math. As I made my way to my desk, I spotted the famed Jack O'Shea. I had to admit, he was handsome. Blonde hair, strands bleached by the sun and starting to grow from summer's crew cut, topped an angular, tanned face. And those eyes. I had never seen eyes that color of blue. Dimples carved into his cheeks as he smiled at me, revealing perfect, Chicklet-like teeth. Oh no, I felt my face flush. Did he notice? He strolled over at the end of the period.

"Hi, I'm Jack O'Shea. You're Kate Gallagher, aren't you?"

I nodded, returning his smile.

"I remember you from math class last year," he continued. "You're one smart cookie."

"Thanks," I mumbled. Why was I letting this guy get to me?

"So, what'd you do over the summer?" he asked, as we walked back to our lockers.

"Not much. Went to band camp. Practiced. Did some reading. Helped around the house. Oh, I did learn how to sew." I sounded so lame. "How about you?" It seemed the polite thing to ask.

"I worked for my dad on some sites around the city. Some of my buddies are into rods, but that's not my scene. I'd rather swim at the Y on weekends. So, you're in the band? What do you play?"

"Flute. I was first chair in junior high. But don't know what'll happen here."

"I'm sure you'll do fine."

Then, it happened. The squealers were lying in wait for him by his locker. The number caught my eye, for some weird reason – number 333.

"Oh, Jack-ee," one started, bouncing up to him. "Have you seen Missy yet? It's such a drag you two were splitsville for the summer. But we're all back together now."

Without saying a word, Jack opened his locker, then looked at me as I made my way down the hall. I could hear the squealing, but not the words – thank goodness.

"I saw you talking to Jack," one of Missy's friends hissed at me as I closed my locker. "Just keep your peepers off him. He's Missy's forever. They'll be jacketed again in no time."

Heat burned from my stomach to my head. How dare this paper-shaker try to tell me who I could talk to. But the last thing I wanted was a cat fight. My fists clenched, I glared at her and turned abruptly, letting my thick, unruly ponytail smack her in the face. Hey, it could have been an accident. I was down the hall and out the door before any more words were spoken.

"Hey, Kate, wait up."

It was Jack. Was he trying to torment me? But I stopped and turned.

"That tail move was so cool," he said, laughing. "I don't know what she said, but she can be bad news with her mouth." He paused before asking, "Wanna go to the soda shop?"

"Sure," I said, and couldn't help the broad smile. He grabbed my books, adding them to his pile.

We talked and laughed all afternoon, about everything and nothing. He really was a good guy.

After several weeks of icy stares from Missy and her crew, they accepted that Jack and I were an item. Nasty comments about our mismatched looks waned. After all, Jack was tall, light-haired, and handsome. I, on the other hand, was a petite brunette. Missy soon turned her flirtations to a junior line-backer, strutting the halls wearing his jacket.

Jack was chosen as the team captain and quarterback of the junior varsity. I placed third chair in the band. We both joined the chorus. We studied together. We made out. I floated on cloud nine. The only darkness came from Jack's home life.

CHAPTER 7

Every family has its problems. I was my mother's.

"Kate, please take your elbows off the table while you're eating. That's better. And sit up straight." How many times did I hear those words? Mother was a stickler for proper etiquette. Thank goodness she had her perfect child in my kid sister, Maureen.

"Kate, must you play those rock-and-roll records so much? All that hound dog music is giving me a headache. And clean up your room – it's a mess."

One of the neighbors ratted me out when her daughter told her I hung around with a hot-rod gang. Mother had a field-day with that discovery.

"What are you thinking, getting involved with fast cars?" she shouted. "You know what they say about girls who hang around those street drag races, don't you? Fast cars attract fast girls. Is that what you are – a fast girl? I raised you better than that!"

I knew Mother would never understand the thrill of hearing the engines roar and the screech of the tires, so I just shrugged my shoulders.

"I saw that look, young lady. Get up to your room, right now!"

Since Mother forbid me from dating until I turned fifteen, I kept my budding romance a secret, meeting Jack after school. He never went to the races with me – it wasn't his scene.

About a year after Jack and I started dating, Mother found out about Jack when Maureen teased me in front of her.

"Well then," Mother said, "when do we get to meet this guy you've been dating? Jack O'Shea, isn't it? I've heard a bit about his family, but your father and I would still like to meet him. Why don't you invite him for supper next Sunday?"

I was a bit nervous the first time Jack came over for supper. Surely mother couldn't disapprove a good-looking, smart, and well spoken young man.

I was wrong. My mother could find fault in anything.

"So, his father's merely a construction worker?" she asked after he left. "I guess that means Jack won't go to college and make anything of himself."

"Mother, his father owns a construction company," I argued. "They have contracts with the city for some major projects. And, Jack is one of the smartest guys in class. He's already looking at colleges. Wants to major in biology. Why can't you, for once, approve of my choices?"

"Because you make so many wrong ones," she replied. Heaven forbid, she should admit to being wrong.

"What?" I asked.

"You heard me. And do not use that tone with me."

"So, I guess it's just not good enough for you that I make good grades. My God, there's no pleasing you."

The argument deteriorated from there, as usual. I ended up running up to my room, slamming the door – as usual.

Jack rarely spoke of his family. I knew he had two sisters and one brother. Colleen was two years behind us in school. And his other siblings were even younger. I'd seen his family at football games, but never gotten the chance to meet them. They always sat together in the front bleachers. I sat in the band section. Once, I worked up the courage to introduce myself after a game. By the time I was within distance of their seats, they had left.

After that supper at my house, I wondered why Jack never invited me to meet his parents.

"We just need to time it right," he explained. "Dad puts in long hours at work. He likes to relax at home. Isn't much for having company."

"Well, I guess that's understandable," I said. "But I'd really like to meet them."

"I just want to make sure everything's perfect when you come over."

Six more months passed.

"Mom's invited you for Sunday dinner," Jack said one day while we shared a frappe. "Can you make it?"

"I'd love to. Plus it'll get me out of listening to my parents drone on about their dull lives. But I better check to make sure Mother hasn't invited company."

The following Sunday, Jack walked me to his house – a white colonial structure, built in the 1920's. It sat in the middle of a block lined with old, gnarled trees amid utility poles, wires, and sidewalks cracked by expanding roots.

Jack introduced me to his parents. His mother stood straight, as if showing off her slim, five-foot-six stature. She was the same height as my mother would be in three-inch heels. Her faded blonde hair, styled in smooth curls, was set off by eyes more turquoise than merely blue. Something in those eyes gave her a fragile, almost child-like bearing.

Jack's father, by contrast, was a large man. Everything about him was nearly over-powering – from his thick stock of salt-and-pepper hair and wide smile, to his broad shoulders, thick arms and beefy hands.

Despite his height and muscular frame, Jack resembled his mother more than his father.

"Well, aren't you just the prettiest thing I've ever seen," his mother trilled. "Why look at those beautiful, almond-shaped eyes. And your skin is so perfect. Oh, to have that again. And you have a widow's peak – how wonderful. Please don't ever cover it up with bangs, dear. Jack, you have such good taste. Just like your father." Her lilting laugh echoed through the room, making everyone join in.

"You're so much prettier than that Missy," Jack's mother continued. "But then, she has those low-class genes from her bleach-blonde mother."

"Now, babe," Jack's father interjected, "let's not go there." Her face transitioned seamlessly from frown to pout, then broke into a generous smile.

"Dinner's about ready," she announced. "Everyone take your places in the dining room. And you all have to clean your plates to get dessert. I made something special."

Mr. O'Shea took his chair at one end of the table, while his wife seated herself on the other end. She insisted I sit to her right, with Jack seated to her left, across from me. His siblings filled in the rest of the chairs.

"I hear you're musical, dear," she said, passing the roast beef.

"Yes, ma'am, I play the flute."

"That's lovely, dear. Jack says you're both in the chorus, too. I'll bet you're an alto. I'm a soprano, but not one of those opera types. Don't think I could shatter glass. Did Jack tell you I used to perform?"

"No, ma'am, I don't think so." I noticed a look pass between Jack and his father.

"Well, it was so long ago. Only a back-up singer. But I worked at The Old Howard. That's how I know Missy's trampy mother." The frown returned, quickly fading into a mournful look. "So sad it's closed now," she whispered. The Old Howard, a burlesque theatre in Boston's Scollay Square, closed its doors in 1953. She looked as if she would start crying. Another look passed between Jack and his dad.

"But babe," Jack's dad quickly cut in, "remember all the great people you met there? And how about the time we saw Sally Keith at the Crawford House? Wasn't that fun?"

"Oh yes … Sally," Jack's mother blurted, giggling and clapping her hands like a child. "She was such a hoot. Boy, how she could make those tassels swing. Much as I tried, I could just never get my – " She stopped, looked around the table at her family, put her hands to her mouth and giggled again.

"Oh dear, I forgot the children were here. Oopsie."

"That's okay, babe," Jack's dad said, smiling. "Girls, help your mother with the dishes." I started to get up. "Oh, not you Kate, you're company."

From the kitchen, Jack's mother was singing "If You Knew Susie" – substituting "Katie" – amid the clatter of the dishes. She had a remarkable voice.

"Jack's quite the player, isn't he?" his dad asked, lighting a cigarette. "He'll be captain and quarterback of the high school team, too. Just like in junior high. There's no one better. And he'll do the same in college. Probably end up a pro."

"Dad, there's more to life than football," Jack said.

"Not for you, boy-o. Gotta use that talent."

"But, remember our deal, Dad. Football now and I can do whatever I want in college."

"Yeah, yeah," his dad replied, dismissively waving his hand. "But football is what'll pay for college. Ahh, here's dessert."

Mrs. O'Shea entered with a tall strawberry shortcake, setting it in front of her husband. She beamed at her masterpiece, nearly skipping back to her seat. Jack's sister, Colleen, placed bowls next to the cake, and then waited while her father cut slices. She carried them around the table, serving each of us a generous portion.

After dessert was finished, I thanked the O'Sheas for the meal and Jack walked me home, holding my hand.

"Sorry about my folks," Jack said, watching his feet, step-by-step.

"I think they're cool," I replied.

"You do?" He looked up, turning to face me as we continued our stroll.

"Yeah. Your mother's a kick, and your dad just dotes on her. They're cute together. Mine are such a drag." We stopped in front of my house.

"Jack, I noticed the look between you and your dad when your mom got sad. What was that about?"

Jack looked down at his feet, then slowly moved his eyes to mine.

"Mom has good and bad moods. Sometimes when she gets sad, she'll stay in her room for days at a time. When that happens, Dad gets angry with life in general. He usually takes it out on the rest of us."

"What does he do?"

"He grumbles a lot. We seem to get on his nerves more. When we misbehave, he lashes out. Mom's not around to get between us."

"D-does he hit you?" I was shocked.

"Not so much anymore. I'm stronger now and I stand between him and the others. He mostly just rants and raves." Jack paused. "But it only lasts for a couple of days. Afterwards Mom comes out of her room, and things get back to normal ... at least until she leaves."

"What do you mean, she leaves?"

"Sometimes when she's really up – you know, real peppy – she just takes off for a few days."

"Where does she go?"

"Dunno. Dad never says. He just goes and picks her up. She comes home, stays in her room for a day or two, then gets back to normal."

"How often does this happen?"

"Oh, just a couple of times a year." Jack stopped talking, looked back at his feet, shaking his head. "I don't want to talk about it anymore."

"Okay. So, what's this thing about football and college you and your dad were talking about?"

"Well, Dad and I do have a deal. I wanna study biology, be a scientist. Contribute somehow. Just don't see doing that playing ball. He agreed if I built up and played the best I can, I could go to college and study whatever I wanted. You know, cookie," he continued, taking both of my hands in his, "we should plan to go to the same school. Whaddya think?"

"That would be peachy," I said, not believing I said "peachy." But I couldn't help it. Butterflies flitted in my stomach.

CHAPTER 8

The spring of my junior year, Mother forced me into a new hair style by directing the beautician on how and where to cut. She wanted me to look like a dark-haired Sandra Dee. But my hair had other designs. I slept in curlers every night trying to tame my natural curls into sleek, soft waves. As soon as any humidity hit my hair – like when I walked out the door – the frizz started. Smooth waves became ringlets sprouting in every direction. Poodles had better cuts. The only satisfaction was in knowing some part of me finally won a battle with mother.

"Cookie, you know I think you're the most," Jack said the first time he saw my new hairdo. "But what's with your hair?" My lower lip trembled. He took me in his arms, cooing that it would be fine – he liked my wild, unruly look. Luckily, my hair grew fast. By summer, I pulled it back into my usual ponytail, although shorter than before.

Jack stayed busy all summer working for his dad. The work was exhausting for him, so we saw less of each other during the weekdays. Friday and Saturday nights gave us lots of time to catch up. We went to drive-ins and dances, or just found a secluded spot to park. And oh, how we made out.

We made it all the way to second base that summer. Parts of my body I didn't know existed tingled every time I saw him. When he touched me, my knees weakened – then a throbbing between my thighs. I'd stroke his leg lightly until he pushed my hand away, groaning. We were madly in love.

In August, our school rings arrived. I wore Jack's, wound with yarn so it wouldn't slip off my finger. The ring made it official – we were going steady.

As his dad predicted, Jack was named quarterback and captain of the football team. Girls swooned and flirted with him. He'd smile politely, and gently let them know he had a girlfriend. I walked taller, smiled broader wherever we went. I doodled hearts in my notebooks, writing our initials inside. Groovy stuff.

Determined to get into a good college, Jack and I studied together at the library nearly every afternoon after football and band practices. The library was a neutral spot – a safe haven from our passion. He applied to several schools, insisting I submit applications at the same time.

I was in a foul mood, matching the dreary, New England fall weather – overcast skies that held a chill portending the upcoming winter. Jack hadn't shown up at the library for our Saturday study date. Arriving home, I stomped up the front steps, slammed the door, and nearly ran into Mother. She looked more grim than angry.

"Kate, honey," she said, "I have some disturbing news. Come, let's sit in the living room."

Why was she being so sweet to me? Did she know Jack had missed our study date? My God, did something happen to him? How would she know? Was it my father? Maureen? I found the school principal, Mr. Winters, in the living room, standing by the fireplace.

"Whatever it is, I didn't do it," I said in a weak attempt at humor to mask my nerves. My stomach tightened, heart pounded.

"Kate, I know you and Jack O'Shea are close friends," Mr. Winters began. "I didn't want you to hear this through the grapevine." He paused, cleared his throat. "There's been an accident."

My knees buckled as I sat on the couch. A lump formed in my throat, strangling me, holding back the tears. Ringing in my ears deformed Mr. Winter's words.

"Jack was riding his bike coming from football practice," Mr. Winters explained. "There were police cars down by the Charles River. Jack went over to find out what was going on. The police received a tip that a body had been found in the river. They were dragging the river. Jack was standing by the yellow tape, as close as he could get to the scene." He hesitated, cleared his throat again. "When they pulled up the body, it was his mother."

I heard screaming coming from somewhere – a primordial noise. It lasted forever. Make … it … stop. Mother was shaking me, holding me, rocking me.

"Shhh, dear," she cooed.

"How, how is he? Where is he?" I croaked, tears choking my voice.

"The police took him to Mass General. They've sedated him," Mr. Winters said.

"I have to go to him," I insisted, standing up on shaky legs, pacing the room.

"Kate, you can't. No one is allowed to see him until they've completed their evaluation."

"Here, honey," Mother said, "take this. It will calm you." She handed me one of her pills.

Without thinking, I swallowed it. I sat back down on the couch, sobbing uncontrollably. Mother and Mr. Winters whispered something by the front door. He left.

"Do you want to talk?" Mother asked, sitting next to me. My sobbing quieted, but no words would come out through the tears.

"Let's get you up to bed. Mr. Winters said you don't have to go to school for a few days."

Sleep evaded me. Thoughts about Jack raced through my head. I willed myself to his side. Maybe he could feel me next to him, calming his nightmare. I sang to him, and to myself. The pill finally worked. I slept with tears dampening my pillow.

CHAPTER **9**

I pulled my black dress from the closet.

"Are you sure you want to do this?" Mother asked, from the bottom of the stairs.

"I have to be there for Jack. I can go by myself, if you want."

"Of course your dad and I will come with you," she said, smoothing my hair with her hand.

Walking to the car parked at the curb in front of our house, I shivered. The cloudless sky contrasted my mood. Arriving at Saint Timothy's, I heard the monotone toll of the bell announcing a funeral mass. The stone spires glittered in the sunshine, casting elongated shadows across the walk approaching the church.

I willed my knees not to buckle as I climbed the steps. We headed to the front of the church, genuflecting and crossing ourselves before entering the fourth pew from the front. I had to be as close to Jack as possible.

The church filled with mourners – family, friends, and students. Everyone stood as the coffin and immediate family entered from the rear of the church, following Father John and several altar boys. The smoky incense rose from the clattering *Thurible* as it swung from Father John's hand, assaulting my senses.

My eyes locked on Jack, willing him to look at me. But he didn't. He shuffled, eyes down-cast. His perpetually-tanned face was drawn, ashen. His father's usual confident stride was somehow shrunken. Tears welled in his eyes. Jack's brother and sisters openly wept.

I blocked out the mass, sermon and music as if in a trance. My only focus was on Jack. Through the rote kneeling, standing, sitting, his posture never varied – slumped shoulders, head down-cast. While his father's and sibling's shoulders heaved up and down with their sobs, Jack's never moved. His bearing didn't alter during the recessional, either. More shuffling. My heart ached for him.

We lined up for the caravan to the cemetery. The seemingly endless line of cars drove solemnly through familiar streets. People on sidewalks stopped, crossing themselves. Entering the cemetery, the procession wound along the avenues lined by massive maple and oak trees, their red, orange and yellow leaves gently fluttering.

I looked around at the people standing by the open grave, coffin suspended above the mound of dirt. Classmates gathered together, with one exception. Missy stood by her parents. Her mother's platinum hair contrasted sharply against the black-attired mourners. The dark sunglasses hid any expression of grief. Missy's father stood stoically tall, as if guarding the grave from unwanted spirits. A gust blew his fedora to the ground.

As he stooped to pick it up, I noticed a bandage on the back of his head. His eyes shifted around the crowd, perhaps wondering whether anyone noticed. Rather than be targeted by his wandering gaze, I looked past him to the trees lining the cemetery drive. I noticed several police officers standing off from the crowd, watching the mourners. The flying hat caught the attention of one officer. He exchanged glances with Missy's father, and then nodded. I turned my attention back to the coffin.

I could stand it no longer. I had to be close to Jack. Weaving my way through the mourners, I stopped next to him. I reached out for his limp hand. It was cold, eerily devoid of life. I intertwined my fingers in his, leaned my body into his, hoping my warmth would penetrate his consciousness. He didn't budge or even acknowledge my presence.

At the end of the service, a relative announced that everyone was invited back to the O'Shea's house. I gently pulled on Jack's hand, leading him away. After several yards, I stopped and turned to face him, taking both of his hands in mine. I bent under his face, forcing his eyes to look at me. They stared blankly.

"Thank you for coming to the service, Kate," his father said, gently replacing my grasp with his own. "I'm sure it means a lot to Jack." He led Jack to the limo.

"Are you sure you want to go to their house?" Mother asked when we returned to the car. "Jack must still be medicated. Otherwise, I'm sure he would have reacted to you."

"Yes, please. Let's go there," I responded sullenly from the back seat.

Tables set with ham, turkey, sandwiches and cookies lined the living room. People milled about, alternately tsking, offering their condolences, and talking about unrelated things. I searched the rooms for Jack.

"I'm so sorry about your mother," I said to his youngest sister, folding her small frame into my arms. "Where's Jack?"

"I think he's up in his room," she said through tears. "Maybe you can get through to him. It's the second door on the right."

I softly knocked on the door. No answer. I slowly turned the knob and entered. Posters and pennants lined the walls, accentuated by his football-themed bedspread. Jack lay on the bed, staring at the ceiling, hands interlocked behind his head. I lay down next to him, on my side, draping my arm around his chest. No reaction. I softly sang to him. "You are my sunshine, my only sunshine."

After what seemed an eternity, Jack's head turned, facing me.

"Kate, I'll always love you," he said, his voice unusually thick and slow.

"I'll always love you, too." I felt elated. I had finally broken through to him. The elation was short-lived. Slowly, Jack turned his back to me, drawing his knees to his chest.

"I'm tired now. Please leave."

CHAPTER 10

" **S** ays here she was murdered," I said to Mother the morning after the funeral. "Strangled before being dumped in the river." I could hardly believe what I was reading in the newspaper. According to the article, the police were questioning several suspects. It hinted Mr. O'Shea's business had possible ties to the Irish mafia. And wrote about Mrs. O'Shea's past as a vaudeville performer in Scollay Square. Everything about the O'Sheas seemed sensationalized. Anything to sell a paper.

Jack never returned to school our senior year. I endured the whispers that suddenly stopped on my approach. I immersed myself in my studies, determined to get into a good college. Maybe Jack would join me there and we could forget this year – get on with our idyllic lives.

A couple of weeks after the funeral, I spoke to Jack's dad. There had been no improvement in his condition. Finally, out of desperation, Jack was admitted to Danvers State Hospital for treatment. Convinced I could bring him out of his funk, I visited him every weekend.

From the time I was a kid, I purposely drove Mother crazy with my antics.

"You're going to drive me to Danvers," she would say, half-kidding, half-serious. Her taunt seemed surreal now.

The first time I drove up to Danvers was nerve wracking – the scenery driving north on Route One reminiscent of a Norman Rockwell painting. Brush strokes of Autumn's colors, dotted with white and brown buildings, twisted with black streets. I could see the hospital, sitting atop a hill, for miles. Salem, with its legends of witch burnings, neighbored Danvers, reminding me of the once unforgiving Puritan influence in New England.

Looking up at the imposing brick institution with its Gothic peaks and spires, the hospital resembled more a medieval nightmare than a castle. I shivered as I drove up the narrow, winding drive to the main gate. I stopped at a small gatehouse, giving the guard my name to gain admittance to the fortress. The tall, iron gates, rusty with age, stood like sentries. Swinging open, the hinges moaned and shrieked their resistance.

Once inside the gates, my fears were abated by the gardens. Neatly trimmed boxwood-hedged mazes formed the backdrop to puffs of yellow, red and orange mums. Freshly dropped multi-colored leaves from the massive trees scattered the manicured lawn like the first rain drops spilled on dry pavement.

I shuddered as I got out of my car in the parking lot reserved for visitors. The crisp air swirled, forming mini-tornadoes of leaves. Blood-curdling screams and inhuman noises from somewhere inside the building sliced through the air like the scraping of metal chair legs on a tile floor.

Jack resided in Grove Hall where patients moved about more freely than in other buildings. Approaching the building, I quivered at the shadows gyrating across the walk and steps – long fingers painted by the nearly bare branches of maples.

Once inside, my nostrils flared, then constricted, at the mixture of ammonia and human waste. The nurse in charge of Jack's ward greeted me.

"Please try not to look alarmed," she said in hushed tones. "We don't want to disturb any of the patients."

"But they're already disturbed," I refrained from saying. She noticed me looking around the hall at the paintings hung on the walls. Odd art works – some almost child-like, others more surrealistic.

"They're done by the patients," she explained. The smile plastered on her lips contrasted the decor of smudged green walls and cracked linoleum floors. "They also paint impromptu murals in the wards," she continued, leading me to one of the gardens.

Jack sat on a bench, alone.

"Hey Jack," I said, sitting next to him, "I brought the newspaper. Thought we could read the funnies together." Jack and I both enjoyed the comics pages. It was always the first part of the paper we read – a similarity we discovered when we first started dating.

No reaction from Jack, so I read them to him, describing every frame as I read the narrative. I'd chuckle from time to time, hoping to get at least a smile in return. Nothing. He just stared straight ahead. That first visit was my shortest, and, I think, most heart-breaking.

"I've decided to be Jack's private tutor," I announced to my parents at Sunday supper. "I don't want him to fall behind his classes. Since he's mostly interested in Biology, I'm going to start reading to him from that textbook. I just know he can hear me. Maybe it'll get through to him."

My parents couldn't mask their pity.

"And stop looking at me like that," I said, angry tears breaking my voice. "I've got to do something for him."

For the next three months, I read to Jack for hours each Saturday, Sunday and holiday break. I started with our high school biology text, and then I moved onto chemistry. I visited a local college campus and bought a text on anatomy. The reading had an extra benefit for me as I advanced beyond everyone in school in those subjects.

As each week progressed, I had more and more "students," as other patients pulled up chairs, or sprawled on the floor, listening to my lessons. I think they just liked the sound of someone reading to them. From time to time, one of the patients would shout out a word, and then get stuck on it like a skipping record. I learned to ignore the distractions. My focus was on Jack.

"You really need to let me know if you're hearing any of what I'm reading," I said one Saturday. "Just blink, or nod, or something." No reaction. Out of frustration, I threw the book at Jack. It bounced off his shoulder, thudding to the floor. The only reaction came from several of my other students. One jumped up, running in circles. Another "eeked," before scooting to the other side of the room. A third patient picked up the book, started to hand it back to me, and then threw it at Jack. Still no reaction. He sat in the chair, eyes staring at the floor. Exasperated, I left, knowing I would continue to visit him whenever possible.

"Kate, may I speak to you for a moment?" one of the doctors asked when I arrived for a visit in February. He led me into an office.

"I'm afraid I have both good and bad news for you," he continued.

"Has something happened to Jack?" I asked, the air in my lungs suspended.

"Actually, yes. And that's the good news."

I exhaled, not realizing I had been holding my breath.

"W-what's happened?"

"He's had a breakthrough. When his dad was visiting him the other day, he spoke for the first time since coming in here. His dad flagged down a nurse, who came and got me. I immediately took them into a private room. He didn't talk much then, but I've been working with him every day since."

"What did he say?"

"I'm afraid I cannot discuss that with you." He hesitated, cleared his throat. "And here's the bad news." More throat clearing.

"Kate, you cannot visit him anymore."

"What? Why not?" I didn't know whether to scream or cry. I was on the brink of both.

"When a patient starts making progress, like Jack, our policy is to limit visitors to the immediate family only. And even their visits are limited. I'm afraid if you want to communicate with him now, you'll have to send messages through his father."

Devastated, I sat speechless. I felt sick. The room blurred. The doctor handed me a glass of water. I drank it, and my head cleared.

"C-can I see him one more time?" I asked. The doctor sighed.

"Okay, but only for a short while."

I found Jack sitting in his usual spot, still that blank stare in his eyes.

"Jack, the doctor just told me that I can't see you anymore," I blurted. "I know you can hear me, dammit. Look … at … me!"

His gaze turned to my eyes. I nearly cried.

"I love you, Jack O'Shea. No matter what, I'll always love you. Please come back to me."

CHAPTER 11

"Honey, you have to get on with your life," Mother said when I returned from my last visit to Danvers.

"How can I when all I think about is Jack?" Tears streamed down my face.

"I know, I know," she cooed, her arms wrapped around me. "It doesn't mean you have to forget him. But he would want you to move on, continue your plans."

"Don't talk about him as if he's dead," I screamed, pulling out of her embrace. "We made those plans together. How can I do them without him?"

"Maybe you can major in something you learned out of this experience. You enjoyed teaching him. Maybe you can be a teacher."

"Oh please, Mother! You know I'm no good with kids. Heck, I couldn't even stand baby-sitting for the neighbors. Maureen is much better at it."

"Then, how about nursing?"

"Oh, right! You know the sight of blood makes me sick."

I remembered an incident when I was a kid. Mother was changing a bandage on my leg from one of my tree-climbing accidents. As she pulled off the bandage, the wound started bleeding and oozing puss. I promptly passed out. Even the thought of it now made me queasy.

"Well, I'm sure you'll think of something."

Later that week, I wrote a letter to Jack and trudged through the snow to the O'Shea's house. A cop car was pulling out of the driveway. Blood pounded in my ears. Mr. O'Shea turned toward the house, not seeing me coming down the sidewalk.

"God-damn cops," he shouted, face flushed. "Couldn't find a fuckin' cat perched on the bottom limb of a fuckin' tree."

I walked up to him, pretending I hadn't heard his outburst. The look on his face when he turned jarred me. Eyes at half-mast, jaws clenched, vein pulsing in his right temple. I saw the temper Jack faced when his mother retreated to her room for days at a time.

"Mr. O'Shea, w-what's happened? Is it about Jack?"

"No, Katie," he said, shaking his head. His hair was mostly salt now, little pepper left. He seemed thinner. He swallowed, sighed, and blinked, trying to control his anger.

"They just stopped by to let me know they still have no leads about Julia's murder," he continued. "They've closed the case, called it a Cold Case." He half-turned to the house, cursing under his breath. I cleared my throat to draw his attention.

"Oh, sorry Katie. I'm a bit distracted. Is that something for Jack?" he asked, noticing the envelope in my hand.

"Um, yes. I wrote him a letter since I can't see him anymore. Will you give it to him? How's he doing?"

"Of course I'll give it to him. His progress is very slow. Sometimes I think it's better for him to stay shut down. At least then he doesn't have the nightmares. I'm sorry you can't visit him, but the doctors say it's the best for him." Again, a heavy sigh. He took the letter and slowly walked into the house.

After brooding for several weeks, taking solace in music, I made some decisions. I knew I needed to get away from the area – it would only painfully remind me of the dreams I shared with Jack. My grades made me eligible for most colleges. The acceptance letters rolled in.

"I've decided to go to NYU," I announced to my parents. "I'm going to major in psychology and minor in music."

"Are you sure you want to go to New York?" Mother asked. "It's so dangerous. And what an odd choice for your major. What on earth do you think you'll do with it?" Mother criticizing my choices meant life was getting back to normal.

"When I used to visit Jack at Danvers I noticed how the patients reacted to different types of music. I thought it would be interesting to actually study the effects of music."

"Okay, but you'll never find a job paying anything in that field."

I sighed. No sense arguing with her.

The remainder of my senior year passed in a blur. Summer, too. I tried getting in touch with Jack several times, to no avail. Around May, his father patiently told me Jack wasn't in any condition to talk to anyone outside the family. He asked that I stop calling.

In late August, I headed to New York City and a new beginning. Five years would pass before I heard from Jack again.

CHAPTER 12

" **C** ome on, Kate, let's get over to the coffee house before all the good seats are taken." My roommate at Judson Dorm, Marylou Turner, exuded more enthusiasm for the "beat" scene than she did for her studies. But then, she was naturally brilliant, requiring little effort to maintain a 3.5 average. Her long, straight dark hair accentuated her lanky body. Her long nails, alternately polished dark red or bright pink, drew the attention of nearly everyone when she dramatically raised them to click her fingers loudly at poetry readings and folk songs.

"Okay, okay," I said. "Just let me get my beret on at the right angle." Marylou rolled her eyes at my constant attempts to include style with the "beat" look.

Along with its abundance of coffee houses, New York was a Mecca for music lovers. Jazz clubs set the cadence around West 52nd Street. Doo-wop bands churned out smooth quartet-style harmonies in the subways and local nightclubs. Dylan Thomas, with his folk tunes and wild hair, frequented the White Horse Tavern and haunted the streets of the Village. Occasionally, we went to an off-off Broadway play at Caffe Cino.

I dated guys of all musical persuasions, and had the wardrobe to prove it. Brad was my sullen beatnik. Joey, with his slicked-back hair, favored the doo-wop scene. Carl was my very own Dylan Thomas look-alike. But none of them could erase my feelings for Jack.

That first Christmas, I carefully wrapped Jack's presents – an NYU sweatshirt and the newest record albums from some of the top bands. His sister, Colleen, answered the door.

"Merry Christmas, Colleen. Is Jack around?" I tried to sound light-hearted, but the knot in my stomach tightened as I saw her expression.

"I'm so sorry, Kate. I guess you haven't heard. Jack's in California."

"California? What's he doing there? Isn't he coming home for the holidays?"

"He left last summer to visit my aunt in San Francisco. He's decided to go to college out there, and will spend the holidays with her family."

"College? He's going to college?" I blurted. "But he never returned to school our senior year." I felt my face flush as I realized how insensitive I sounded.

"One of his teachers tutored him so he could graduate," she explained.

"Can I write to him? Or maybe call him to wish him a Merry Christmas?"

Colleen hesitated, cleared her throat, looked down at her feet. Mr. O'Shea appeared at the door, and Colleen faded into the house.

"Katie, I'm so sorry," he began. "Jack's still a bit shaky. He went to California to get a new start. Doesn't want any reminders of what's back here – the memories, or nightmares. I can let him know you stopped by, but I think it's better if you don't try to get in touch with him. Please, Kate, for your own good – let him go."

I stood frozen at their doorstep, clutching Jack's packages. Tears trickled down my cheeks. I didn't wipe them away. I simply handed the presents to Mr. O'Shea.

"Here. These are for Jack," I whispered, choking on the words. I could think of nothing else to say, and needed to get away from the pity openly displayed on Mr. O'Shea's face. I turned and ran back to my house, slammed through the front door, and ran to my bedroom. I took turns sobbing and cursing for hours. Finally, I set my jaw and stared at my image in the mirror. I was determined it was the last time I would cry over Jack O'Shea.

The next three-and-a-half years sped by, as I alternated between immersing myself in my studies and partying as wildly as time permitted. After the events of that first Christmas, I lost my interest in psychology. On the advice of my guidance counselor, I switched my major to music education.

By my senior year, drugs were rampant in the Village, and students were starting to rumble about "the establishment." I wanted to embrace it all. Marylou actually did. One scary night of watching her as she tripped on God-knows-what, I decided hard drugs were not my scene. I tried Mad Dog at one party. After puking my guts out the next day, I was done with wine. I preferred reefer and good ol' PBR – Pabst Blue Ribbon. I could live with the belching and munchies just fine.

After graduation, I returned to my parents' house while searching for a job. One afternoon, I saw a familiar face on the street.

"Missy? Is that you?" I asked. Always so perceptive. She was pushing a stroller, with a toddler hanging onto her skirt.

"Kate. How good to see you. I heard you graduated from NYU and are back at your folks."

"So, are these your kids?" Well, duh.

"I guess you've been out of contact. Yep, they're mine. Bobby and me got married right out of high school. You know … young love, and all that crap." She hesitated, and then continued. "Speaking of young love, do you ever hear from Jack?"

"No," I said plainly. "The last I heard several years ago was he moved to California."

"It's such a shame what happened to him. He had such a bright future ahead of him. But my mom says it's really no surprise what happened to his mom."

Dumbfounded, I stared at her. Why would she say such a horrible thing? Taking my silence for some cue, she continued, her rambling defying interruption.

"You know, my dad dated Jack's mom before he met my mom. Probably the worst fights they ever had were over her. Then, after the funeral I just never heard either of them mention her again. Sorta weird, since they fought about her every couple of months. I finally asked Mom about it a few years ago. She told me that with her quirky ups and downs, and running around with undesirables, it was no wonder she got herself in a bad situation. Mom said she felt sorry for Mr. O'Shea for having to put up with her for so many years." She finally took a breath.

"Well, I always found her to be nice," I said. "Frankly, Missy, I can't believe you would say such rotten things about Mrs. O'Shea. What happened to her and her family was a tragedy." At that, I turned and walked away.

"Someday you'll find out the O'Shea's aren't so great," she shouted to my back. "The truth will come out. You'll see."

CHAPTER **13**

I landed a job at the South End Music School, giving private and group lessons. Since I had a passable voice, I taught both flute and voice. The job actually gave me some sense of accomplishment, plus paid enough for me to move out of my parent's house to a third-floor walk-up, one-bedroom apartment not far from the school. Furnished with bedroom furniture from my parent's house, and a couch and tables from a local thrift store, it reeked bohemian.

In my spare time, I embraced the music scene in Boston. Doo Wop music morphed into an almost preppy type of rock-'n-roll, captured by notables like The Beach Boys and Simon and Garfunkel. Motown grew in fame. The Beatles started the British invasion. I still preferred jazz, but grew to appreciate more popular bands, especially under the influence of good ol' reefer.

For the next two years I blissfully floated through life. I visited my old roommate, Marylou, a couple of times in LA. She had transcended the beat scene to hippyism, a true follower of "Flower Power".

One night in 1965, while enjoying my favorite jazz band at a Boston club, a shiver ran through my body. It wasn't the music, but something else emanating from my soul. Suddenly, I started crying. The explanation came a week later with an unexpected phone call and a letter that changed my life.

"Hey, Kate. It's Colleen O'Shea."

"Colleen. Jeez, I haven't talked to you in ages. How's it going?"

"Not so well. Are you sitting down? I'm afraid I have some bad news. It's about Jack."

Knees suddenly rubbery, I plopped down on the couch – breath suspended in my throat.

"I don't know how to say this other than just blurting it out." Colleen paused, a quiet sob escaping. "Jack's dead."

"What? How?" My ears started ringing, stomach flip-flopped.

"Vietnam." Her one-word reply spoke volumes.

"I-I didn't even know he was over there," I stuttered.

"He signed up right after college, went through officer training, and headed out." Another pause. "You know Jack. Always wanted to make a difference. ... He didn't suffer."

"Colleen, I'm so sorry," I mumbled, tears trickling down my cheeks.

"Anyway, we're having a small service for him," Colleen continued. "Dad thought you might want to come."

"Of course I will."

The following Saturday, I walked up the steps to Saint Timothy's. Memories of his mother's funeral flooded my mind. Jack's father and siblings quietly sobbing. The procession of the casket, this time tended by soldiers. Hearse, limo and a few cars meandering through the streets to the cemetery. People along the way crossing themselves. The mellow resonance of a lone bugle playing "Taps," contrasted by the staccato of the three-volley gun salute. The invitation to join the family at their house.

"Katie, thanks for coming," Mr. O'Shea said, as I entered the house. I hardly recognized him as the once tall, proud, broad man I'd first met so long ago. His hair, now completely grey, topped a face lined by too much tragedy.

"A letter came in the mail a few days ago," he continued. "It's for you, from Jack." He led me into his office, handed me the envelope, then quietly left, closing the door behind him.

I stared at the envelope, written in familiar script. Hands shaking, I carefully opened the flap, and unfolded the letter. Blinking away tears to clear my vision, I read his words.

> *"My dearest Kate:*
>
> *If you're receiving this letter, it means I didn't make it back from Vietnam. I needed you to know that I never stopped loving you. In fact, I loved you too much to put you through a life of misery. I told the doctors at Danvers to keep you away. I wanted you to get on with your life. I saw what my dad endured for years with*

mom. I knew I'd never be completely sane – just like her.

I've kept track of your life, and am so proud of your accomplishments. I wish I could have shared them with you, like we planned so many years ago. Instead, I can share only one part of me – a legacy to everything we meant to each other. I don't know whether you'll accept it, or not. Your choice.

Enclosed is a round-trip ticket to San Francisco and a contact point at Cal State. Dr. Epstein was my professor, mentor and friend. He will explain every-thing to you.

Please forgive me, Kate.
My love forever, Jack"

The letter floated to the floor. I leaned into my hands, moaning, rocking, crying uncontrollably. I thought I shed my last tear for Jack years ago. Straightening up, drying my eyes, I resolved to take the trip to California. Somehow, I knew my future would forever be tied to Jack and his legacy – whatever that was.

CHAPTER 14

"Dr. Epstein? I'm Kate Gallagher," I said, entering his office, hand extended. He wasn't what I expected. Rather than an Einstein look-alike, Dr. Epstein was around 40, medium height and build, balding. His broad smile instantly comforted me.

"Kate. Why you're lovelier than your pictures. I can see why Jack was enraptured. Please, have a seat." He cleared a stack of papers from a chair, setting them on the floor. His office was cluttered with books, files and papers strewn haphazardly across his desk, chairs, file cabinets and book cases. The only bare oasis in the paper jungle was the center of his desk. Posters of anatomy parts dotted the walls. Cleanliness under the pandemonium was evidenced by the absence of odors – only the nutty aroma of coffee.

After the preliminaries about my flight and hotel, Dr. Epstein cleared his throat before talking about Jack.

"Jack was an exceptional young man. He had his darker moments, but he'd get through them by immersing himself in his studies and lab work. Didn't make many friends. Almost as if he feared any closeness. Then, one evening, when he was in the lab after classes had ended, I approached him. He wasn't too talkative at first, but finally opened up to me after several months. He never really got over his mother's death, or that her murder was never solved." Dr. Epstein lowered his head, gently shaking it from side to side before continuing.

"I'll tell you, Kate, whenever he spoke about you, I saw a certain light in his eyes. I tried to encourage him to contact you, but he refused. Got rather stubborn about it. So, I dropped the subject. Then, he somehow felt honor-bound to join the Army after he graduated. I tried to dissuade him. Even suggested the Peace Corps instead. He just wouldn't listen. God, he had a pig-headed streak."

"So, what is this 'legacy' he wrote me about?" I asked, gently trying to get to the heart of our meeting.

"I've been doing some work on artificial insemination," Dr. Epstein explained. "It's been around for centuries – mainly in animal reproduction. But since the first U.S. human insemination in 1953, hundreds of women have taken advantage of the procedure."

What did this have to do with me? or Jack? Forcibly containing my fidgeting, I silently waited as Dr. Epstein continued.

"Jack was helping me out with my research when the idea came to him."

"What idea?" I had to ask.

Dr. Epstein cleared his throat, looked down at his hands folded in his lap. When he returned his gaze to me, an unexpected thrill ran through my stomach – like the feeling you get when looking over a steep cliff.

"He had his sperm frozen," Dr. Epstein blurted. "It's for you, Kate."

My mouth opened and shut, no sound escaping. Spots formed before my eyes. I stared at Dr. Epstein, listening through a tunnel.

"I know it's very unconventional, to say the least," Dr. Epstein said. "But Jack thought it was his best way of sharing his love with you if he didn't return from that damned war. I like to think if he had returned he would have gone to the ends of the earth to get you back. You know, don't you, he wasn't really crazy. He thought he'd somehow inherited his mom's illness. I tried to tell him it was nonsense. He was as sane as I am." Dr. Epstein chuckled, and then leaned into me, concern furrowing his brow.

"Kate, are you okay?" he asked.

The posters blurred. Mounds of papers and books undulated oddly, like broken waves slapping a sandy beach. I looked at Dr. Epstein, a tunnel blocking out everything but his face. I passed out.

When I came around, Dr. Epstein offered me a glass of water before explaining the process. I didn't understand all the details, but got the gist.

"Take your time and think about it, Kate. You don't have to give me an answer right now. After all, the sperm aren't going anywhere." He chuckled.

I wore the nubs off the carpet in my hotel room that night, pacing back and forth. On the one hand, I could have a part of Jack with me forever. Would it be a boy or girl? Or twins? Heaven forbid. Would it look like him? What? Was I nuts? I couldn't take care of a baby. I didn't know how. But then, is any first-time mother prepared? It could have his incredible blue eyes I could stare into every day. Would I take his name? No. We were never married. It wouldn't be right. Hell, we never even had sex. How weird is that? A baby with no consummation. I giggled.

There was no one I could call to talk it over. Mother would have the vapors. I giggled again at the vision of her collapsing into a chair, fanning herself. I sobered at the thought this was my decision alone.

I finally slept. I dreamt of Jack in our better days. Then of his vacant eyes while at Danvers. Suddenly, cutting through the vision, I saw his eyes meet mine, dreamingly sparkling. He smiled and spoke.

"I love you, Kate. You're strong. You can do this – for both of us." His face stayed with me as I jerked awake.

The next day, I contacted Dr. Epstein to arrange the procedure. I never regretted my decision. Seven months later, I prematurely gave birth to a beautiful baby girl. She had the eyes Jack inherited from his mother – more turquoise than merely blue.

PART THREE

ALEXA

"Well, Alexa, that's pretty much everything there is to the family history," Nana Kate said, reaching over to pat my hand. "Have I totally freaked you out?"

"Sort of. But let me get all this straight. Julia O'Shea, my great-grandmother, was murdered in 1958, and dumped in the Charles River. My grandfather, Jack, saw his dead mother on the riverbank, and went bonkers. Then he was killed in Vietnam, but had his sperm frozen before going there. Wow, what a family." I shook my head in amazement.

"A bit blunt," Nana Kate said, a well-manicured finger punching the air, "but accurate."

"I'm still confused about one thing though. What month was it when Jack died?"

"July," Nana Kate replied.

"So, if you were inseminated in August," I said, mentally calculating the months, "then mom would have been born in May. But her birthday is in March. So you should have gotten pregnant in June. That's a month before Jack was killed." I strummed my chin, shaking my head. "It just doesn't add up."

"Your mom was two months premature," Nana Kate explained. "It actually worked out perfectly. Anyone doing the math would think she was conceived in the more traditional way. In fact, my mother concocted a story that Jack and I got together before he shipped off for Vietnam. She wove in the hint of passion fueled by him going off to war, and how we planned to get married when he returned. Her cronies ate it up, remembering what it was like during World War II. I went along with it, of course. Not for my sake, but for your mom's."

"So Mom really was a virgin birth. How cool is that?"

"Hey, I was hardly a virgin," Nana Kate chuckled. "I slept with plenty of guys in my day – some more special than others. And they all told me how great I was. If I had looser morals, I could have made a living that way. Boy, I know some tricks. I could teach them to you, if you want. I know we have a banana in the kitchen."

TMI – too much information. I was torn between putting my fingers in my ears and chanting la, la, la, la, or running into the kitchen to fetch a banana.

"Kate," Mom screamed, face flushed. "We really don't need to know any of this."

Nana Kate winked at me. She always seemed to know what I was thinking and enjoyed pushing Mom's buttons. I stifled a giggle.

"Are there any clues at all as to who killed Julia?" I quickly asked, getting us back to the subject at hand.

"None I know of," Nana Kate said. "I remember Jack's dad being so frustrated with the police at the time. And the newspaper articles insinuated that somehow the Irish mob might have been involved. I'm afraid I just didn't know all that much about Julia, or what she did when she disappeared for days at a time."

"How about we delay any guesses until we get a look at the case file," Mom suggested – always the voice of reason.

"Wait a minute," I said. "What do you mean 'we'? This is supposed to be my project for course credit."

"Oh, but what a great idea," Nana Kate piped in. "Of course, it would still be your project. But you could deputize your mom and me to help out. We haven't had a good family project since we made root beer."

What a disastrous end to that experiment – bottles exploding in the basement like live grenades. What a mess.

"This isn't exactly like mixing up some syrup, water and sugar," Mom cut in. "It's much more serious. And Alexa's right. It is her project. If she wants our help, she knows where to find us. We'll just hang out here and be supportive. After all, she may not even want to take this case as her project." Big sigh, perfectly-coiffed blonde head bowed.

Oh god, she was playing the mother's-guilt card.

"Okay, okay," I said, folding the hand I was dealt. "Let me first take a look at whatever is in the archives, and then we'll go from there."

"Oh goodie," Nana Kate said, clapping her hands. Mom slyly grinned as I inwardly groaned.

The next day, I announced my decision to Ryan and Frank.

"That's an awful old case, Callahan," Frank said, twirling a toothpick around in his mouth. He had an endless supply of toothpicks. "Chances are, whoever did it is dead. Sure you don't wanna tackle something a bit newer?"

He had a point.

"I thought about that." I stood and strolled over to Frank's desk. An advantage of my height, even in strolling mode, only three steps took me to my destination. "But I figure this is primarily a project for credits in school, so it's not really critical we put someone in jail for the murder. It's more about finding and following clues to unravel the puzzle. Sort of honing and showcasing my investigative skills."

"Plus the family factor," Ryan added.

"Yeah," I conceded. "But think about how much you can teach me." I was tempted to flutter my eyelashes.

"You don't have to flatter us to get our help," Ryan said, smiling. God, he had a dazzling smile.

"Come on, Callahan," Frank said, rolling his chair back. "Let's get over to the archives."

I refrained from saying, "Goodie," and clapping my hands, like Nana Kate.

CHAPTER **16**

"**O**kay, sign here," the keeper of the archives said dryly. The box was covered with years of dust. I sneezed three times. No one bothered to bless me.

The number on the box caught my eye – 58-0333. Three threes. Now I knew it was meant to be – this case had been sitting on a shelf waiting for me to solve it. I lifted the lid, startled by the contents.

"There's not much here," I said. Ryan and Frank peered in over my shoulder. Frank grunted.

Back at the office, I plopped the box on a work table and slowly examined each piece of evidence, checking it against the yellowed, brittle roster. Nothing missing. I scanned the investigative report, short as it was.

I carefully read the interview reports. The cops had talked with Julia's husband and children, except Jack. There was a note explaining Jack was not able to give a statement due to his commitment to Danvers. No shit. There were statements from some of the neighbors, a couple of Julia's friends, and Mr. O'Shea's coworkers. A tattered flowered dress was crumpled in an evidence bag, as was a faded scarf, marked as the suspected murder weapon. The autopsy report listed the cause of death as strangulation. No lab report on the scarf or dress. This would be a challenge, alright.

"So, do you think the lab will run a DNA test on the dress and scarf?" I asked Ryan.

"I don't think that will give us any answers," Ryan said. "In the first place, any useful evidence was probably washed away while she was in the river, and then caught on the bridge abutment. Secondly," he held up two fingers now, "you need to get a sample from any suspects for the lab to match against your non-existent evidence. And thirdly, we don't even know if we'll find any suspects or whether they'll be alive."

"Okay, so that's a dead end," I conceded, sighing. "I'm just not sure where to start here. Mind if I brainstorm with you guys a bit?"

"Proceed," Frank said, leaning back in his chair, toothpick in place. He really belonged in a Dashiell Hammett novel – more Sam Spade than Nick Charles. His toothpicks replaced the hand-rolled cigarettes. I half expected him to call me, "doll-face."

"Okay," I began, fingering through the items in the box. "We have a dress and a scarf." I paused, thinking. "But where are her other clothes? No shoes. No undergarments. The shoes might have fallen off, but the panties, bra, and hosiery wouldn't. So, those items might have been dumped somewhere else." I re-read the investigative report. "There's no mention of them here. Curious."

"Anything in the interviews?" Ryan asked.

"Let's see. Mr. O'Shea said Julia had gone on one of her adventures into Boston a few days before she was found. He didn't know exactly where she had gone. Said she normally ended up at Joe's Diner, where he'd pick her up. He didn't give much else. I can understand that. Hell, he was mourning. Plus, Julia was his wife. He certainly wasn't going to start rattling on about her to anyone." I paused, reading through the other interviews again.

"It looks like the kids didn't know anything more. God, this must have been hard on them." A pang of sympathy fluttered in my stomach.

"A couple of neighbors seemed to just speculate," I continued. "People do like to gossip. I guess they must have been the source of the juicy stuff that ended up in the papers." Scanning the interviews, a page caught my attention.

"Here's one from a guy who worked with Dan. A Mr. Greg Lyons. Says he went to see Mr. O'Shea at his house the night of the seventeenth. Mr. Lyons had seen Julia at a place called The Club. She was leaving with a man named Nate Jamison. When he told Mr. O'Shea, they argued. Mr. O'Shea told him to mind his own business, and then slammed the door in his face." I looked at Frank.

Feet propped on his desk, crossed at the ankles. He grunted.

"What?" I asked. "This ring a bell with you?"

"Not saying yet. Just continue."

"What's the report say about how the body was found?" Ryan asked.

"Let's see," I said, summarizing the report. "On October 18, 1958, at two fifteen in the afternoon, a Mrs. Williams approached a cop saying she saw something floating in the Charles River, at the Longfellow Bridge. The cop, Henry Monroe, went with Mrs. Williams to take a look, and determined it was a body stuck on a bridge abutment. He then radioed the department. A team of cops was sent to the river, including a diver who went in to retrieve the body. She was sent to the morgue, where they identified her as Julia O'Shea."

"Who were the investigators?" Frank asked.

"There's a William Deavers and Edward Jamison," I said after looking at the report. "Do you know either of them?" I paused, recognition slamming my brain. "Jamison's the last name of the guy from the interview."

"Heard of Deavers, but he's dead," Frank said. "Jamison must have been fairly new to the force at the time. He retired about fifteen years ago. Still lives somewhere in the area."

"So, is there a connection to the guy from the interview?" I persisted.

"Eddie was old man Nick Jamison's nephew," Frank explained. "We all knew Nick. He was quite the dandy in his day. Always wore a fedora and dressed to the nines. A lady's man, flirting with anything in a skirt. He was some hot-shot at one of those insurance companies. Word is he drank himself to death about twenty years ago." He paused to change toothpicks, and then continued.

"Nick's wife was a piece of work. When I first started on the force, I found her drunk and disorderly in a local bar. I was gonna bring her in, but my partner explained to me who she was, so we just escorted her home." He shook his head. "I musta escorted her at least a dozen times while on that detail."

"So, what kind of cop was Eddie?" I asked.

"Eddie was a good enough fella, but lacking in the brains department," Frank said, chuckling. "We useta joke that when God was passing out brains, Eddie thought he said 'trains' and said, 'no thanks, I'll walk'." Ryan and I snickered.

"I really think Eddie was just lazy," Frank continued. "While the rest of us would be bustin' our humps to solve a crime, Eddie was in charge of fetching coffee. But he did have his uncle's gift of gab. Always volunteered to interview the

71

women on any case. He never seemed to get any information, but did get a lotta phone numbers. Sometimes I think the only reason he never got canned was because of Nick."

"What do you mean?" I asked.

"Nick was smart. Didn't get to be an executive without knowing what's what. He useta take Eddie out to lunch now and then – especially when Eddie seemed stuck on a case. When Eddie'd get back from eating, he always seemed to have new ideas on how to look at the case. Plus, Nick had social connections with some of the power-brokers in the city. Played golf with 'em, went to some of their shindigs. He just had to keep a tight leash on his wife when they went out so she wouldn't embarrass him." Frank paused again, thinking.

"You know, now that I'm talking about it all, I do remember something weird happening at his funeral. Nick's wife seemed to be half in the bag by the time everyone got to the cemetery. I woulda thought she was just on some sedative, since she was in mourning. But I was close enough to her that I could smell the booze on her breath. Anyway, just as the priest was finishing his last blessing, I heard her mutter, 'Save a place for me in hell, you bastard.' Then, she turned around and was starting to walk to the limo when she suddenly stopped, looked down at another tombstone, and let out this spine-tingling shriek. Her daughter – I think her name was Missy – rushed to her side, put an arm around her shoulders and had to nearly drag her to the limo. Mrs. Jamison was muttering something the whole time. It was just so odd." Frank shook his head.

"So, how does all this get us any closer to Julia's murder?" I asked.

"How long was the investigation open?" Ryan asked. I looked down at the report, mentally calculating the dates.

"Looks like only a couple of months."

"Well, I don't know how good of an investigator Deavers was," Frank said, "but that seems about par for the course for Eddie."

"Which means?" I prodded.

"There may be much more to this case than is in that box and report," Ryan answered.

CHAPTER 17

Ryan and Frank returned to piles of paperwork on their desks. I started taking notes on the contents in the box and what I had learned from our brief brainstorming session. Twirling the ends of my hair with my fingers – a habit I picked up when I stopped biting my nails at the age of twelve – I reviewed my notes and charts.

Point one – Julia O'Shea was strangled to death with a scarf. Where was she killed? Why did the killer use a scarf and not his or her hands? Maybe whoever it was didn't want to leave any prints. That could mean it was pre-meditated, which ruled out a crime of passion. But if it was planned, then why not use a gun or knife? No, strangulation usually indicated an impromptu act.

Point two – Julia was found in the river. Assuming the killer dumped her there, it had to be a man, or a very strong woman. How did she get from where she was killed to the river? Or was she killed near the river and dragged into the water? Nothing in the report about footprints or drag marks near the scene. But with the tidal movement in the Charles River, couldn't she have been dumped at some other point, and drifted to the bridge abutment? Maybe the killer thought the tide would take her body out to the ocean, not counting on it running into the bridge. Why didn't the killer weigh down her body? But then, it wouldn't move with the tide.

A look at the coroner's report yielded a bit more information. No one questioned the missing undergarments. Why would the killer remove them? I found it unlikely Julia would willingly go anywhere without being fully dressed. Her time of death was estimated at between ten PM and five in the morning – a window based on the tides. High tide was around eleven fifteen PM, and low tide was around five forty-five AM. If the killer intended to have the body drift out with the tide, then the timing made sense. There were no marks or bruising on her to indicate she had either jumped or been thrown from the bridge, which meant she was somehow placed in the river. The only scrapes on her body were caused by colliding with the bridge abutment. Decomposition and bloating were minimal. No prints on the scarf, dress, or body. There was no mention of scrape marks on her feet or legs to indicate the body was dragged. Did the killer carry her from where she was strangled to the river? Again, had to be either a man or very strong woman. I was going with a man.

"How come there are no lab reports?" I asked Frank.

"Well, we may have a world-class police lab now," he said, "but it wasn't around until about forty years ago. Didn't have one back then." He looked back down at some paperwork shuffled on his desk. I stared at my notes.

The big mystery loomed – what was the motive?

I squeezed my eyes shut, massaging my temples. Too many questions rolled in my brain. I played with an idea that may lead to more headaches.

"Hey Ryan," I said, swiveling my chair to face his desk. "I have an idea that might help move this along."

"Let's hear it."

"My nana and mom grew up in this area. Nana Kate knew some of the people who were interviewed and is familiar with things from back then. Plus, mom was an investigative reporter for years. How about I bring them in to take a look at what's here?"

"It's your project ... and your family." As he turned to Frank, I noticed the uplifted corners of his mouth and the eye-roll. He was amused by my idea.

"Hey, I saw that look," I said, annoyance adding an edge to my voice. "Are you guys patronizing me? If so, then just stop it. Yes, this is a project about a family member. But it's also a cold case that none of you sharp-witted detectives could ever solve. What, are you scared some college intern will show you up and actually solve it?" I was on a roll. Then I looked at Frank. Reddened face, narrowed eyes. I braced myself for the blast of steam building in his head.

"Steady now," Ryan walked over and put his hand on Frank's arm.

"Look, Alexa," he continued, hands lifted in surrender. "We are professionals who do take your case seriously. I'm just not so sure it's a good idea to bring in your mom and grandmother.

We're here to help you out. Do you really think they could add anything?"

"You may be right," I half-way conceded. "But I know they'll bug me about it, so I figured it might be easier to just let them sift through what's here. Of course, I would want you guys here, too. I really do value your input." Okay, I was on an about-face roll now.

Frank grunted.

"Just remember, you're in control of the case, and be careful," Ryan warned. "Keep their imaginations under control. Stay with the facts, use your investigative instincts, and what you've been learning."

I turned to Frank, hoping my doe-eyed stare would have the same affect on him as Nana Kate's had on me.

"Bring'em on," he muttered. "But first, you'll go with us to wrap up another case. It'll give you some experience you may need on yours. We have an appointment in an hour."

CHAPTER **18**

"So, how old's this case?" I asked as we headed to the car.

"Goes back to ninety-two," Frank said. He pulled out the remote, clicking it twice to open all doors. I sat in the back seat of the navy sedan, equipped with all the bells and whistles needed for communication and high-speed chases. Since it was rarely used for transporting prisoners, there was no cage between the front and back seats.

"What's it about?"

"You're too young to remember, but there was a big celebration that summer. A bunch of tall ships came into the harbor. Lot of 'em docked at the Navy Yard in Charlestown. Nightmare for the police. Thousands of locals, tourists, and crew cluttered the city. I pulled duty around Quincy Market. Lotsa drunk and disorderlies, but nothing we couldn't handle." Frank shook his head.

We entered the Navy Yard, turning left on First Avenue, creeping by buildings new and converted since the closure of the Yard in 1974. Condos, apartments and small businesses took advantage of the Yard's proximity to Boston. Glancing to the right, I stared at the USS Constitution, its masts proudly jutting above the Inner Harbor, a tribute to the hundreds of warships built in the Yard since the Revolutionary War.

"What're we doing here?" I asked.

"Scene of the crime," Frank said, bluntly.

We dead-ended at Sixteenth Street. Beyond a vacant lot, the Mystic River ended its journey into the Inner Harbor.

Getting out of the car, Frank led the way to the lot.

"Right over there," he pointed about ten yards ahead, "cops patrolling the Navy Yard found the unfortunate victim, one Billy Cronin."

"He was shot point blank, right here," Ryan pointed to the center of his forehead.

"The cops narrowed it down to three suspects," Frank continued. "Unfortunately, all three had air-tight alibis. Ryan, please do the honors of summarizing the suspects."

"First, we had Sean Casey," Ryan said, his index finger raised. "Tough guy. Always getting in fights. Hot tempered. Witnesses said they heard Sean and Billy get into it in Clancy's Pub the night prior. Something about Sean owing Billy some money. A couple of punches were thrown before the bartender threw them out. Sean's girlfriend vouched for his whereabouts at the time of the murder. Said they were together all day and night, enjoying the weekend festivities." Ryan paused.

"Our second suspect was Tim Matthews." Ryan held up a second finger. "Tim and Billy were best friends since high school. Played ball together. But one of their other friends said Tim and Billy had a falling out. Apparently, Tim made a pass at Billy's girlfriend, Betsy. She denied it, of course. Said Billy was always thinking guys were coming on to her. Said they'd patched up their differences. But jealousy can make a sane man crazy. About a week before the murder, Billy did a number on Tim. Beat him up pretty bad. But Tim had an alibi, provided by his mother."

"And our last suspect was Gary Samuels." Ryan's third finger appeared before he dropped his hand. "Gary worked with Billy at some auto shop. Claimed Billy stole some tools from his bin. That's big money to mechanics. Plus the ethical issues. Billy denied it, of course. The shop owner looked into it, and found out Gary was lying, trying to get Billy fired, to steal his customers. The owner ended up firing Gary. His alibi was the weakest. Claimed he was at some big party. Several people saw him there, but couldn't substantiate when he left."

"What about the murder weapon?" I asked. "Any prints, or other DNA evidence?"

"He was shot with a .45," Frank said. "The weapon was never found. No casings to recover with a revolver. Ballistics wasn't much help without the weapon. At least not back then. Nothing was left behind to run through the lab. Too many footprints in the area to identify which belonged to Billy or his killer."

"So, who's your best guess as the killer?" Ryan asked.

Pacing in circles, I silently reviewed Ryan's descriptions. All three had motives, and all had alibis. Maybe not the most reliable alibis. But there you have it.

"With what you've told me," I concluded, "I'll go with Sean Casey. Having a girlfriend vouch for him isn't very strong. If they spent the day enjoying everything going on with the tall ships, it puts him at the scene of the crime. He could have scoped out this spot. Seems pretty secluded. Then he lured Billy here with the promise he'd give him the money he owed him."

"Okay, then," Frank said, walking back to the car. "Let's go visit Billy's mother to give her the news."

"What? Wait a minute," I whined. "You can't base anything on what I just said, given the sketchy information you provided."

"Don't worry, Callahan. Got you covered."

Leaving the Navy Yard, we drove several blocks before parking in front of a brick row house. An elderly woman met us at the door. Frank handled the introductions. Mrs. Cronin invited us into her living room.

"You said on the phone you've figured out who killed my Billy," Mrs. Cronin said, wringing her hands in her apron.

"Yes ma'am," Frank said. "Arrested him this morning. Got him to confess."

"Well, who was it?"

"Tim Matthews."

"No, it can't be," Mrs. Cronin said, shaking her head. "He and Billy were best friends." Her hands shot up to her mouth, as tears coursed down her plump cheeks. Wiping her eyes with the hem of her apron, she croaked, "Tim married Betsy a couple of years after Billy died. Have a couple of kids. They visit me at least once a month. How could he have done such a thing?" She searched each of our faces for an answer.

"You remember Billy beat Tim up pretty bad, don't you?" Ryan asked. Mrs. Cronin nodded. Ryan shrugged. "Everything will come out in the trial, Mrs. Cronin. We're so sorry for your loss." As she collapsed into a chair, face buried in her hands, rocking back and forth, we left.

"My God, that was heart-wrenching," I said from the back seat. "Poor woman. And hey, why didn't you tell me you knew who the killer was? You're not trying to make me feel dumb, are you?"

"Nope," Frank said, pulling into traffic. "So, why don't you tell me again why you concluded it was Sean,"

"Based on what Ryan told me, he seemed to be the only one with motive, means and opportunity. He had fought with Billy about money. We could place him near the scene of the crime earlier in the day. And he had a way to lure Billy to the Navy Yard. Plus, having a girlfriend vouch for him was weak."

"And why did you eliminate Tim?"

"He had an alibi."

"Provided by?" Frank asked.

"His mother."

"And you don't think she'd lie for her son?"

"I guess I just assumed she'd tell the truth," I conceded.

"Assumptions, Callahan. Avoid them like the plague." Frank's toothpick swirled.

CHAPTER 19

"So, we finally get to meet Frank and Ryan?" Nana Kate asked when I told them about going to work with me the next day.

"Please remember, they reluctantly agreed to this," I whined.

"Don't worry, honey," Mom said, patting my hand as if I was a four-year-old, "we won't embarrass you ... will we, Kate?" Her stern glance at Nana Kate left no room for negotiation.

The next morning, I was pleasantly surprised when I entered the kitchen. Mom and Nana Kate, dressed in conservative skirts, blouses and pumps, could have posed for the fashion section of *The Boston Globe*. Both attractive women, Mom stood three inches taller than the petite Nana Kate. They had kept their figures over the years. I felt an odd surge of pride in my lineage, although the resemblance was slight. Nana Kate was maybe five-three, with dark hair sprinkled by strands of grey, and hazel eyes. Mom's golden blonde hair had faded over the years, but was still striking in its smooth page-boy style. Her blue eyes startled anyone seeing her for the first time. I was the tallest of the trio, attributed more to my dad's lineage than Mom's. Although blonde, I had inherited Dad's brown eyes. The only resemblance between the three generations was our mouths – corners uplifted at the end of full lips.

Heading to the car, I noticed Mom's brief case.

"What's in there?" I asked.

"Just a notebook and some pens."

"Mom, we have plenty of those at the station."

"But you wanted us to look professional. I thought this completed the look." Always the height of fashion.

"Maybe we could pick up some pastries on the way to put in your case," Nana Kate suggested.

"No," I said firmly. "Let's just leave the food and brief case behind."

As we entered the office, Frank and Ryan politely stood, making their way over to us. Ryan smiled, while Frank kept his usual dour expression. At least he didn't have a toothpick swirling in his mouth. I hadn't been this nervous since introducing my first date to Dad. I held my breath as Nana Kate extended her hand to Ryan.

"You must be Ryan," she said demurely.

I exhaled, relieved her proper-lady persona was present.

"And you're Frank. It's a pleasure meeting both of you." Looking directly at Frank, she continued, "I appreciate this opportunity to help out. And thank you for agreeing with Alexa on her choice of cases to work. It really means a lot to our family to finally find out what happened to Julia." Her eyes actually moistened. The doe-eyed look was genuine, void of any mirth.

Frank smiled shyly – an expression I hadn't seen him wear before. "My pleasure, Mrs. Gallagher."

Nana Kate brought out a side of Frank that I, frankly, found a bit disarming.

"Please, call me Kate. It's much easier than explaining the non-Mrs. thing."

"Sure thing," Frank replied, turning to Mom. "It's also nice meeting you, Mrs. Callahan. Alexa's a quick study." Man, he was just being so polite. I stared at this usually gruff man, confused.

"Oh, just Lilly, please." Was Mom about ready to bat her eyelashes? Geez.

"Well now, should we get down to business?" Mom asked. "We'll need some paper and pens."

I pulled out the evidence, reports and my notes, neatly piling them on the table. Ryan pulled up chairs for our visitors. During the next hour, Mom and Nana Kate passed papers back and forth – slowly reading, quietly taking notes. Every time I started to interject a comment, Mom held up a finger and shushed me. So, I sat, twirling my hair. With each shush, Frank and Ryan grinned.

"Well, I agree we don't have a whole lot to go on here," Mom said, removing her reading glasses. "It's confirmed this was murder and not some accident … or suicide. I think we should start by making a list of people to interview. Kate, who do you think could give us a bit more insight?"

"It's been such a big family secret for so many years," Nana Kate began. "Kinda like the stinky gorilla in the room. No one ever talks about it, that I know of. But I bet we could get Colleen and Mary to open up … if approached right. In fact it might be a bit cathartic for them."

"Who are Colleen and Mary?" Ryan asked.

"They're Julia's daughters," Nana Kate explained. "There were actually four children. But the two sons are dead now." Eyes cast down, she softly sighed, shaking her head.

"Are you okay, Nana Kate? Do you need some water or something?" I felt her pain at the memory of Jack.

"No, I'm fine, honey," she said, looking up. "Colleen and Mary are in their early and mid sixties now, but I'm sure they remember everything like it happened yesterday. I keep in touch with them from time to time. They could fill in some of the blanks for us. Maybe they even talked to their dad about it before he passed away."

"Well, it's certainly worth a shot," I said, making a note to set up the interview. "Anyone else?"

"If we can find him, Eddie Jamison might be of some help," Nana Kate suggested. "He was a couple of years ahead of me in high school. Dumb as a stump, but with a bit of charm. I went to school with his cousin, Missy. We've never been on the best of terms though."

"I was a cheerleader with Missy's daughter, Kathy," Mom interjected. "We were actually pretty good friends back in high school. I remember she was always so embarrassed by her mother and grandmother. We'd sometimes go to her house to study or just hang out, and they'd be at the kitchen table, half in the bag. The first time I met her granddad was really weird. Kathy and I were sitting in the living room talking when he came in. When Kathy introduced me, he just stared at me. Like he wasn't really seeing me. Gave me the creeps." Mom shivered at the memory. "I used to hear him berate his wife and daughter. Even spoke harshly to Kathy sometimes. But never to me. He always spoke to me in soft tones, almost charming.

"Anyway," she continued, "if we need to find Eddie, I could probably ask Kathy. We don't see each other much anymore, but I'm sure she'd help out."

"I knew her grandfather," Frank said. "Name was Nick Jamison. Quite the ladies' man in his day."

"Well, I don't think he was trying to woo me," Mom said, smiling. Then she rubbed her temples. "Damn, another headache twinge." She grimaced, shook her head, and looked up. "Okay, now who else should be interviewed?" Back to business.

"The neighborhood's changed so much since then," Nana Kate said. "I don't think many people are left from that time. Maybe some of their children or grandchildren are still living there."

"But anything they could tell us would be second or third-hand," I said. "Not very reliable. Mostly gossip."

A pause in our thoughts permeated the room. Frank cleared his throat.

"Some ground rules here," he started. "Alexa needs to be in on all interviews. And either Ryan or I should be there, too. But I see no reason why Kate and Lilly can't help out. Especially with family members. I'll see if I can find out where Eddie's gotten to." I glanced over at Mom and Nana Kate. Mom smiled primly, nodding her head. Nana Kate beamed, smiling broadly. I knew her femme-fatale facade was fading.

Crossing the room, Nana Kate approached Frank, grinning like a school girl.

"You know something nice about getting older?" she asked him. "What used to be considered sexual harassment is now a compliment. I look forward to working with you, Frank." She winked at him. He blushed. I stood there with my mouth open, closed it, groaned, and shook my head.

CHAPTER 20

"What else have we got here?" Mom asked, looking into the box. She pulled out the dress and scarf still captured in their evidence bags. "Think there are any labels left on these clothes that might help out?"

I put on latex gloves before opening the bags. Gingerly, I lifted the items, looking for the labels.

"They're pretty faded," I said. "But I think I remember something in one of the reports about the labels." I thumbed through the paperwork.

Hearing a snap, I turned to Mom. Standing like a surgeon ready to operate, hands lifted in the air, she examined the gloves fitting tightly around her fingers. She reached for the scarf, almost touched it, and then quickly pulled back her hand as if licked by a hot flame. She closed her eyes, opened them, visibly gulped, took in a deep breath, and grabbed the scarf. She stared down, transfixed.

"What's the matter, Mom?"

"I-I don't know," she stuttered. "There's something about this scarf – something familiar, yet I can't remember." Straightening up, shaking her head, she continued, "Oh, it's just one of those déjà vu moments." She put the scarf back in the evidence bag.

"Here it is," I said, looking at the police report. "It says the scarf was a Chanel. Hmm, not cheap. The dress had a label from Filene's Basement."

"I just had a thought," Nana Kate said. "Is there anything in the report about her jewelry? She should have at least had on a wedding ring. But I remember she always wore other jewelry – earrings, and usually a necklace. She really was quite stylish."

"It does mention a wedding ring and small diamond on her left hand. But no other jewelry. I guess they could have fallen off in the river. Or maybe the killer wanted it to look like a robbery. But I can't imagine a robber strangling someone with a scarf. More likely, he'd use a gun or knife. And it says here the rings were given to Mr. O'Shea."

"Well, we're not getting much from the clothes," Mom said as she put them back in the box. "But you never know when the smallest of things lead to something bigger."

"Is there some way we can take a look at what the newspapers said about the murder?" Nana Kate asked.

"We do have access to LexisNexis," Ryan said. "But if you're looking for newspaper articles, you can probably just go to the library."

"Can we do it online?" I asked, figuring you could find anything online these days.

"I think *The Globe*'s online archive only goes back to around 1980, so that's not gonna help out here."

"I have some contacts at *The Globe*," Mom said. "If we can't find what we're looking for at the library, we can go right to the source. Hmm, I wonder if anyone's still around who would have remembered reporting on the case."

We all sat around, silent, except for the light drumming noise from Frank's beefy fingers. He pushed back his chair, stood and stretched his arms above his head.

"Well," Frank said, "I guess we're about done for now. We have some work cut out for us. We need to interview some people and do some research of old newspapers. I suggest doing the research first. Then interview the daughters. We should meet back here every few days to talk about what we found out. Then go from there. Remember … Callahan and either Ryan or me is in on every interview." He paused while partially bowing to Mom and Nana Kate. "Ladies, it's been a pleasure."

PART FOUR

SECRETS, LIES
AND DREAMS

CHAPTER 21

"Boy, I haven't seen one of these things in years," Lilith said, gazing at the library's microfiche reader. "You have to be very gentle with the controls, or the images will flash before your eyes like the white dotted lines on a highway. Here you try." Lilith relinquished the seat to Alexa, and pulled up a side chair. They were starting their search with archived copies of *The Boston Globe.*

"Whoa, baby," Alexa said, as she barely touched the control. "Even a speed reader couldn't keep up with this. I'm getting dizzy." Taking her finger off the dial, she took a deep breath and tried again.

"Okay, I'm looking for October 19, 1958," Alexa said, her tongue peeking slightly from the side of her mouth as she concentrated on working the reader. She paused, searching the headlines. Nothing on the front page, or even the first section. Must have been a busy news day. But then, it was the Sunday paper.

"Here we go," she said, stopping on an article in the Metro section. "A woman identified as Julia O'Shea was pulled from the Charles River by police at approximately three o'clock in the afternoon the previous day. Unidentified sources in the police department confirmed the cause of death as strangulation and not drowning. Hmm. Nothing else here than what we already know."

"Let's switch to *The Evening American*, that's the predecessor to *The Boston Herald.* It was a tabloid and may give us a bit more," Lilith suggested. Alexa switched film slides, and gingerly worked the controls, scanning the articles.

"Here it is," Alexa said. "And you're right about a bit more information. Says Julia was the wife of Daniel O'Shea, and once performed at The Old Howard. Then it goes into more about Mr. O'Shea. Says his construction company was recently chosen to sub-contract on the Charles River development in the west end. The general contractor was associated with Sean

O'Connor, an up-and-comer in Boston's Irish Mafia." She paused in her reading to look at Lilith. "Can they say that? It seems like that kind of statement would be grounds for a liable suit."

"Well, I guess reporting was a bit different back then. What else is there?"

"Not much else. Now what?"

"Let's take a look at other crimes reported on the day she was found," Lilith suggested. "We still don't have a clue as to where and why Julia was killed."

"Why look at that date?" Alexa asked.

"Maybe something happened on the night before she was found that will lead us somewhere."

"Like a robbery, or mugging, or something?"

"Let's not be too narrow in our search, though."

Alexa went back to carefully scanning the microfiche.

"Let's see, there's a burglary on Commonwealth Ave ... a house fire in Charlestown ... a domestic disturbance on Marlborough Street ... a drunk and disorderly at Riley's Pub ..."

"Wait a minute," Lilith said. "Read more about the drunk and disorderly, then the domestic disturbance."

"It says a fight broke out at Riley's Friday night when some guy made unwanted advances to another patron. Police were called by the owner at about midnight, after several patrons started throwing bar stools around the place. Flying debris hit the bartender, knocking him unconscious. Four men were arrested ... Jake Darby, Bill Nelson, Tommy Fitzgerald, and Bobby Dunkirk. Probably taken to the drunk tank." Alexa giggled, picturing a scene from nearly every cowboy movie she'd ever seen.

"Now for the domestic disturbance," she continued. "Police were called by the landlord of an apartment building on Marlborough Street around ten-thirty in the evening of October seventeenth." Alexa paused. "Hmm, that's the same night as the fight in Riley's." She continued reading. "One of the tenants complained they heard a lot of shouting coming from one of the units. When the police arrived, they interviewed the occupants of the apartment, but no arrests were made. It doesn't identify the occupants ... yet it names the landlord and the person who complained. That's odd. You'd think if people were going to be named, they'd give everyone's names."

"The occupants probably had some juice," Lilith said.

"Juice?"

"You know ... pull, or power, or influence."

"I know what it means, Mom" Alexa said. "I've just never heard you use that term. I think you've been reading too many dime-store detective novels."

After printing off the articles they needed, Alexa continued looking through the film, but found nothing else even remotely associated with Julia's death.

"Well, that looks like about it for now," Lilith said as they turned off the reader and returned the films to their envelopes. "We can always come back later to do more research."

"Think it would help to go over to *The Globe*?" Alexa asked as they exited the library.

"Don't think so," Lilith answered. "The library's archives had just as much as the paper's would. I did call a guy I know over there, though. When I told him how old a case this is, he said that any reporters from back then would be retired ... maybe not even alive anymore."

Around two o'clock in the morning, Lilith jerked awake, sitting up in bed. Her heart pounded like a gorilla trying to escape its cage.

"What's wrong, honey?" Bill asked, sleep tugging on his vocal chords. He reached over to rub her back. "Why are you so clammy?" Sitting up next to her, he was now wide awake.

"I-I had that dream again," she whispered. "I haven't had it in about twenty years." She shook her head, trying to sort out the images.

"Maybe it was triggered by your work on this murder case," he suggested.

"I don't know ... that's probably it. But the three men's faces seemed much clearer this time. And there was no floating figure. It ended with the men holding that damned red scarf. I still couldn't make out what the dead woman was trying to say to me before I became her. And this time there was a low, wailing sound in the background just before I switched places with her." She stopped, taking deep breaths to regain her composure.

"Did you recognize any of the men this time?" Bill asked.

"No ... at least not that I know of." Getting out of bed, she turned to her husband. "I know I won't get back to sleep now. I think I'll just go read or something for awhile." She bent down and kissed him.

In the den, Lilith grabbed paper and pen. She'd never had any artistic talents, but her innate ability to recall and describe events had served her well during her career as a reporter. While the images of the three men still floated in her mind, she jotted down their features. Perhaps one day she would meet them and tie up the loose ends of her recurring nightmare.

CHAPTER **22**

"**O**ld ladies love me," Ryan announced when everyone gathered in the office the next day to decide who would conduct their first interview.

"Hey, I can be charming," Frank retorted. Everyone's eyes rolled like saucers suspended on sticks.

"Now, I may think you're cute as a button," Kate said, patting Frank on the knee, "but these ladies may be intimidated by your ... uh ... masculinity. It's probably better to have a less distracting, younger man there." She could really shovel it.

"Well, okay then," Frank grunted.

"Should I be insulted by what Kate just said?" Ryan whispered to Alexa.

"Don't take it personally. She just has a way of getting what she wants," Alexa whispered back.

"Then it's settled," Kate announced, triumphantly. "Alexa, Lilith, Ryan and I will go visit Colleen and Mary. Since they both live in the same town, they're going to meet us at Mary's house. I told them we were coming for two purposes – to have a nice visit with them, and to talk a bit about their mother. They seemed to be excited, especially about getting a chance to see Lilith and Alexa. It's been years since they've seen either of you. In fact, I think Alexa was just a toddler."

Colleen and Mary lived in Chelmsford, about twenty miles north of Boston. Once a quaint New England town, with its historic homes and small common surrounded by family-owned businesses, Chelmsford had evolved into upper-middle-class housing developments. These had sprung up in the eighties when high-tech companies discovered the Route 128 beltway, expanding Boston's suburbia.

Driving up Route 3, Kate revealed part of a plan she had formulated for the interview.

"Lilith, I want you to be the last to enter the house," Kate said. "In fact, you should pretend you left something in the car, so you come in a couple of minutes later than the rest of us."

"Now why would I do that?" Lilith asked. "Does it have anything to do with why you insisted I wear my hair like this?" Her faded blonde hair was styled in soft curls, rather than her normal smooth pageboy.

"I'm not telling." Kate crossed her arms, pouting like a four-year-old.

"No disrespect intended," Ryan said, "but it might help if we all knew your plan."

"I just think it will work better if you don't know," Kate said, unfolding her arms. "Sometimes the element of surprise for everyone works for the better. All I'll say is that you and Alexa should watch the sisters when Lilith walks in the house."

Lilith and Alexa knew stubbornness was Kate's strong suit. She could be charming, playful, or down-right flirtatious when she wanted something. But when all else failed, her heels dug in so far they put an oak's root system to shame.

Sitting on top of a hill in a small housing development, Mary's house was a twenty-year old garrison on a standard quarter-acre lot. Perfect gardens of roses and multi-colored annuals showed off the green-thumb talents of someone living in the house. The driveway curved along the side of the house ending at a two-car garage. Parking at the end of the driveway, Kate, Alexa and Ryan walked to the front door. Before they could ring the bell, Mary opened the door, smiling broadly. Colleen stood slightly behind her sister, arms ready for embracing their guests.

"Come on in," Mary said. "It's been just too many years."

The interior was a wonderful blend of aromas, a tribute to Mary's cooking and cleaning skills – like Mr. Clean was having an affair with Betty Crocker somewhere inside. The sisters were handsome women. Both tall with middle-aged spread around the hips, Colleen had salt-and-pepper hair pulled back in a twist, while Mary's more stylish short hairdo merged brunette and blonde hues.

Once in the house, Kate made the introductions. Colleen and Mary cooed when they met Alexa, giggling and hugging her like a mama bear with a cub who had wandered too far from its den. They blushed as Ryan flashed his brilliant smile.

"Where's Lilith?" Mary asked, peering outside toward the car.

"Oh, she forgot something in the car," Kate replied. "I swear she'd forget her head if it wasn't attached. She'll join us in a minute."

"Well, let's go sit and have a nice visit," Mary said. "I'll leave the front door ajar."

Moving from the brightly-lit front entry toward the living room, their chatter was interrupted by a soft rap on the front door.

"Hello there," Lilith called. "Mind if I come on in?" As she crossed the doorway, the light filtering into the entry softly backlit her silhouette.

"Oh, holy Jesus," Colleen whispered, crossing herself. She staggered over to the door jam, leaning on it for support. Turning quizzically to her sister, Mary looked to the front door to see what had evoked Colleen's reaction. Staring at Lilith, her hand shot to cover her mouth. Her lips began to quiver before a sob involuntarily escaped.

Ryan, Alexa and Lilith briefly glanced at each other, then the sisters, and finally at Kate – wondering what was happening here. Noticing that Mary and Colleen were about to collapse, Ryan and Alexa helped the sisters to chairs in the living room.

"Mary ... Colleen, this is Lilith," Kate announced once the ladies were settled.

"My God, Kate, she looks exactly like Mom," Colleen said, regaining her voice. "I-I thought I was seeing a ghost."

Kate barely disguised her knowing smile as she winked at Alexa and Ryan.

CHAPTER 23

After the initial shock of seeing a vision of their mother, Colleen and Mary settled into the role of hostesses, offering a variety of non-alcohol drinks and tea sandwiches. The living room was a tribute to Mary's style with a floral couch set off by two winged-back chairs, both covered in solid colors from the couch's background. Striped drapes carried the color scheme to the windows. Pillows carefully placed on the couch and chairs balanced the flow of hues. The cherry-stained coffee table and end tables matched the wood revealed on the chairs' arms and legs. The furniture was neatly arranged to focus attention on the marbled fireplace.

"Well, I'm sorry," Mary said, looking at her glass of tonic water, "but I need something stronger than this. Anyone else?"

"I'll have whatever you're having," Colleen said. Mary walked over to the buffet in the adjoining dining room and poured a healthy shot of vodka into their tonic waters. Everyone else kept with their soft drinks.

"Ahh, that's better," Mary sighed, after taking a generous gulp from her drink. "Now, what's this about looking into Mom's death after so many years?"

"I started it as a project for school," Alexa began. "But the more I look into this family mystery, the more intrigued I get." She paused. "Does Mom really look like Julia?"

"Oh honey," Colleen answered, "she is the spitting image of my mom. I knew Lilly always resembled my side of the family, but now that she's about the same age as mom when she died, the resemblance is almost uncanny ... or maybe spooky is a better word."

"I'm sorry I startled the two of you," Lilith said. "I really had no idea. You see, we don't have any pictures of your family." She looked over at Kate, raising an eyebrow, akin to pointing a finger at the guilty party.

"Okay, okay, it's my fault," Kate said, raising her hands in fake surrender. "I've watched Lilith grow into a woman with all of Jack's features. To be honest, my memory of Julia isn't crystal clear ... more like flashes of images. I remember how she used to wear her hair, her trim figure, and her lovely singing. I was working on a hunch that Lilith looked enough like Julia to stir up your memories. I don't know a lot about her to help out with this case. We're all hoping you can fill in some details to lead us in the right direction." Then Kate remembered her manners.

"By the way," she said, looking from Colleen to Mary, "I'm so sorry about Tommy's accident." Tommy, Jack's younger brother, had been killed in a car accident several years earlier. Both sisters thanked her, and then crossed themselves.

"So, can you tell me a bit about Julia?" Alexa asked the sisters, bringing them back to the purpose of the visit. "I hope you don't mind me calling her by her first name, but that's how I think of her."

"No, we don't mind, dear," Mary answered. "After all, you didn't know her. Plus it might keep everything less confusing for you." She drained her drink, mixed another for both sisters, and sat back in her chair. "Let's see ... how to describe Mom. My, so many memories flood my mind ... of both good times and bad. I was the youngest of the four children, and only eleven when Mom was murdered. Such an ugly word – murdered.

"Mom was a complex woman. She certainly loved her family. In fact, she doted on us kids, always bringing us back little presents from her trips."

"Come on, Mary," Colleen interrupted, swigging back the last of her second drink. "Let's be honest here. It's not going to help anyone by continuing the fantasy Mom took 'trips'." She made quote marks with her fingers when she said "trips." She'd been fifteen when her mother's death relegated her to the role of woman of the house – watching her younger siblings, fixing dinner, cleaning and cooking.

"Mom was what today would be termed bipolar," Colleen explained, looking at Alexa. "In her manic times, she was the life of the party. So much fun to be around. Played with us for hours on end. Then the chemicals in her brain would shift, and she'd retreat to her room for days at a time. I remember once, we decided to try to snap her out of the doldrums by putting on a little skit. I think I was about eight at the time. Jack was ten, Tommy six, and Mary four. We planned to sing a medley of children's songs – 'Mary Had a Little Lamb', 'Itsy Bitsy Spider' and 'Row, Row, Row Your Boat'." She paused in her memory. "I don't know why I'm remembering this now. I haven't thought about it for years." Another pause. "Anyway ... we were halfway through the spider climbing up the spout, when Mom started crying and ordered us out of her room. We never tried to cheer her up again."

The room fell silent, allowing Colleen time to calm herself.

"I remember Jack telling me your mom would go off some-where a few times a year," Kate said, bringing them back to a crucial topic for the case. "He never knew where she went. Just said your dad would go and pick her up, and then she'd go to her room for several days. I'm now assuming she'd take off dur-ing one of her manic periods. Right?"

"We never did know where she went when we were kids," Colleen answered. "But Dad finally talked about it some years later. It's almost like he finally needed to let go of all the family secrets. Anyway, he said she still had cravings for the limelight. She was never a star performer when she worked at Scollay Square, but always had dreams of being center stage. She'd wander off a few times a year to hang out in bars in Boston – finding places where she could sing. I asked him one time whether she was with other men during these times. You have to understand, he loved her dearly. But he wasn't blind ... or stupid. All he said was she always attracted men because she was so beautiful. He never admitted she was unfaithful."

"How did she get into Boston when she'd take off?" Alexa asked.

"She had a car back then," Colleen said. "But she never took it. She'd take off while we were in school and Dad was at work, so we never saw her leave. I can only assume she took a cab or the trolley."

"Did your dad ever mention the names of bars where she went?" Alexa asked.

"When they were first married, they used to hang out at The Red Hat and the Old Brattle Tavern. I'm not even sure if they're still around. After all, it's been fifty years since mom died. Chances are pretty slim any of her old haunts exist. Or if they do, they've probably changed hands several times."

"Yeah, you're right," Alexa admitted. "I'm stumped at how to figure out where she went, or who she met. There's got to be some link between these wanderings and her death."

"Wanderings. I like that term," Mary said, nodding. "Mom was on one of her wanderings when she was killed." Mention of the word "killed" acted like a vacuum, sucking all air from the room. For the first time that afternoon, Julia's death was referred to as something other than just a death. Everyone sat, transfixed.

"Let's try something else," Ryan suggested, breaking the spell. "How about we look through some old pictures, if you have any. Maybe we'll see something in them to point us in a helpful direction."

"Besides which," Lilith added, "I think it's about time I got to see what your side of my family looks like."

"Well, I keep all the old pictures in my hope chest," Mary said. "Somehow I ended up with all the family's pictures. Come on, Lilith, help me dig them out."

"Mary ended up with all the family pictures because she's the only one with any organizational leanings," Colleen whispered to Kate, rolling her eyes. "She's got them all in albums. Geesh. Did you get a look at her gardens? Such the perfectionist."

"It's said a picture is worth a thousand words," Lilith said, following Mary into the den.

CHAPTER 24

L ilith and Colleen lugged several photo albums into the living room. Categorized by time, Colleen first opened an album starting in 1954. Everyone gathered around the large coffee table.

"You know, Dad was quite the picture buff," Mary explained. "He had that damned camera with him everywhere we went. Thought it was funny to catch us in embarrassing situations. See here? That's one of me kissing a poster of some movie star. I had such a crush on him. I remember being mortified Dad snuck into my room to take the picture." She paused at the memories. "But I guess I'm glad now, since we have so many photos from back then."

"Here's one of Jack in his junior high football uniform," Colleen said, pointing at a good-looking, tall young man holding a helmet. "He was handsome, wasn't he? Dad was so proud of him."

"My God, Mom," Alexa said, looking at the picture, "he looks a lot like Johnny."

"That's your brother, isn't it?" Mary asked.

"Yes, it is. He's sixteen. Looks like Mom. I take after Dad."

"Why didn't you bring him along?" Colleen asked.

"He's at baseball practice," Lilith answered, noticing Colleen's disappointed look. "But I promise you'll get to meet him soon." They resumed looking through the pictures.

"Here's one of Mom, Mary, Tommy and me cheering Jack on at some game," Colleen said. "Boy, I had a big mouth, didn't I?"

"Oh, ugh," Mary said, pointing to another picture. "This must be from some big junior high dance. That's the horrid Missy Jamison with Jack. Boy, I just couldn't stand her."

"Yeah," Colleen added, "I remember one time in high school, when she sashayed up to me and announced that if she wanted to, she could take my boyfriend away from me like that." Colleen snapped her fingers. "It was my freshman year, and I was dating Bobby Nichols. Missy was a junior, and of course, a cheerleader. Bobby was a linebacker ... also a junior. He was good-looking, but not the brightest bulb in the circuit. Anyway, she went after him, just to prove her point. Since everyone knew she put out, it didn't take long for Bobby to succumb to her charms. I wasn't too broken up about it. She ended up getting pregnant at the end of their senior year, so they got married. I heard since he never got a chance to sow his wild oats before getting hitched, he ran around on her all the time. Goes to show that you get what you pay for." Colleen chuckled.

Flipping through the album, Mary came to pictures from 1958.

"Here's one of Mom," Mary said. "See how much you look like her, Lilith?" The resemblance was remarkable. "And here's one of Jack and Kate before their junior prom. What a lovely couple. Here, let me give you this one, Lilith." Mary pulled the picture out of the album and handed it to Lilith. Kate looked over at the picture, smiled and sighed.

"Are you okay, Kate?" Lilith asked.

"I'm fine, honey. It brings back some wonderful memories."

"Oh, and here's a rare one," Colleen said, turning to another page. "I don't know who took it, but it actually has Dad in it. He was so muscular back then."

"Can you take it out of the album so I can get a better look at it?" Lilith asked. Mary gingerly peeled back the plastic covering and handed her the picture. Putting on her reading glasses, Lilith moved over to the lamp to study the picture under better lighting. She gasped ever so slightly.

"What is it?" Kate asked.

"I-I don't really know," Lilith stuttered. "There's just something oddly familiar about him. When was the last time I saw him?" She looked at Kate.

"Let's see ... he died around 1970, right?" Kate's head turned to Colleen, who nodded. "So, you would have been fourteen. I remember taking you to the hospital to see him before he died. But he didn't look anything like this." Kate pointed to the picture. "In fact, he got grayer and leaner year by year after Julia died. I don't think you ever saw him looking this strong. I doubt you would remember him like this." She handed the picture back to Lilith.

"Wait a minute," Lilith said, grabbing her purse. Since taking notes on her dream, she carried the descriptions around with her, hoping for a chance meeting with the men who held the scarf.

"Listen to this, and tell me whether it sounds like him. A tall man – maybe six feet or a bit more – dark, thick, straight hair, parted on the left side; light eyes, either blue or green; straight eyebrows; nose that appears to have been broken – kinda like a boxer's, but not as squished; faded scar on his right cheekbone; broad, muscular build … especially his biceps; and a tattoo of some sort on his left forearm." Lilith put down her notes and looked up a Colleen and Mary. The sisters stared at each other, confused.

"That's a good description of Dad," Mary said. "He got into some bar fights in his younger days. Got his nose broken and never had it fixed. Made him snore like a freight train." She winced.

"I remember the day he came home from work with a big gash on his cheek, up near his eye," Colleen continued, pointing to her right cheekbone. "Mom was so upset. She drove him to the hospital to get stitches. And he had a tattoo of a woman on his forearm. He claimed it was Mom." She paused before asking, "How did you know all this? What're those notes?"

"Back when I was in my teens and early twenties I used to have this recurring nightmare," Lilith said. "It came to me again the other night. I got up and took notes on what I could remember, including the descriptions of three men in the dream." She described her dream to everyone.

"I don't put any real power in dreams," Ryan said. Alexa scowled at Ryan, keeping her lips tight. "But it gives us a bit of something to go on," he continued. "Let's take a look at pictures from earlier days, and work our way forward. Maybe these other two men are in there somewhere."

Mary pulled out an album from her parent's younger days. They flipped through several pages, not recognizing all the people in the pictures. Lilith sat right in front of the album, carefully searching the faces.

"I don't know who half these people are," Colleen explained. "I guess they were friends of Mom and Dad. If we need to know, I think Dad was pretty good about putting names on the back of them."

"Wait. Stop," Lilith said, staring and pointing at one picture. "Who are these people with your Mom?"

"That's Nick and Rosie Jamison," Colleen said. "I remember them from when I was little. There's quite a story that goes along with them."

"Do tell," Lilith prompted.

"Well, Mom and Rosie worked together at The Old Howard. I guess they were pretty good friends at one time. Even talked about forming a singing duo. Mom dated Nick, until she met Dad. She told me one time, that after Dad swept her off her feet, she broke up with Nick. He moped around for a little while, and then started dating Rosie. He was trying to get back at Mom for breaking up with him. I guess they still remained friends, of sorts. Hell, Mom didn't care he dated Rosie. In fact, she was glad he moved on. But then, she started hearing he was moving on with more gals than just Rosie. She tried to tell Rosie about it … big mistake. That's when they had their falling out." Colleen pointed to the picture as she continued.

"Musta been after this picture was taken. Rosie accused Mom of being jealous and wanting Nick back for herself. After Mom and Dad got married and Mom was pregnant with Jack, Rosie got knocked up by Nick to get him to marry her." Colleen chuckled. "I guess like mother, like daughter. Anyway, it didn't stop Nick from stepping out on Rosie. Every now and then, I'd see him at football games, always wearing that damned fedora. A regular Dapper Dan. He was actually pretty nice. When Jack and Missy started dating in eighth grade, I remember him coming up to Mom and saying something like, 'Funny how they ended up together. I guess the attraction has moved forward to the next generation.' Hmm," Colleen stroked her chin, eyes lifted toward the ceiling. "Then Mom said something I forgot until now. She said, 'Some attractions are just timeless.' Then she giggled. Kinda odd, now that I think of it."

"But she never liked Missy," Kate said. "Or at least that's what she told me."

"No, she didn't. Missy looked just like her Mom … didn't have any of Nick's features. Mom told me one time she wasn't even sure Missy was Nick's kid. Rosie did her bit of running around, too. I think in a way, Mom felt sorry for Nick."

Lilith looked down at her notes, reading her description of another man from her dream. Shifting her eyes from the picture to her notes, back and forth, she recited aloud what she had written. Colleen agreed the description sounded like Nick. Lilith glanced at her own forearms, covered with goose bumps. Two down, one to go.

CHAPTER 25

Mary turned the album pages more slowly now, as Lilith scrutinized each picture. None of the males in the pictures came close to the description of the third man from her dream.

"Oh, we're in the birthday section," Mary said, looking at pictures of cakes, children with party hats, and scenes of games.

"Here's one of me playing the piano at one of Jack's birthdays," Colleen said, pointing to a girl of about eight, sitting on a stool. A cake celebrating Jack's birthday sat on a table in the foreground. "I never was any good. But Mom insisted someone in the family had to play. She wanted it for when she broke into song. Tommy started playing when he was about four. Mom was convinced he was some sort of virtuoso. He was good ... much better than me. But since he was only thirteen when she died, she never got to hear how really talented he was." She sighed at the memories.

"Who's this guy?" Lilith asked, pointing to another picture.

"Umm, let me think," Colleen said, squinting at the photo. "Oh yeah, that's some guy who worked with Dad. Rather homely, isn't he? I remember he was always hitting on Mom."

"Oh, was that the guy who used to corner Mom by the fridge?" Mary asked. She shuddered as she stared at the pockmarked face. "He gave me the creeps. What was his name?" She gingerly pulled the picture from the album, turning it over. "Oh, here it is. Greg Lyons."

"Can I take a closer look?" Lilith asked. Mary handed her the photo. Lilith stared at the image of the man standing next to Dan. They were about the same height, but Greg's waistline out-measured Dan's by at least ten inches. Portly. His ruddy, scared face was accentuated by the bulbous nose of a man who liked his drink. Curly, brown, unruly hair fell into eyes at half-mast. Lilith checked her notes. He didn't match any of the descriptions from her dream.

"So, he worked with your dad?" Lilith asked, handing the picture back to Mary.

"Yes," Colleen responded. "I remember Mom and Dad talking about him. She always tried to avoid him. Didn't like him. Dad said he was harmless. Used to laugh that Greg was a wanna-be mobster."

"How so?" Alexa asked.

"I guess he was always picking fights. Mom finally banned him from the house after he took a swing at someone during one of our parties."

"Do you know what ever happened to him?"

"I heard he died about ten years ago." Colleen paused in thought, eyes roaming to the ceiling. "I think he was killed in a car accident. Probably drunk."

"We can check it out," Alexa said, jotting a note.

They continued flipping pages of the album.

"Hold it there," Lilith said as Mary turned another page. "Who's that guy? I haven't seen him in any other pictures." She pointed to a man sitting at the piano, Julia standing next to him, mouth open in song.

"Hmm, I don't remember," Colleen said. She took the picture out of the album and turned it over. "It says here his name was Tony Bronkowski." She handed the picture to Lilith, who walked over to the lamp and held the picture under the light.

"Looks like he was younger than Julia," Lilith said. "Are there any other pictures of him in there?" Mary scanned the next couple of pages before finding another picture with Tony. She removed it and handed it to Lilith.

Quickly grabbing her notes, Lilith alternated between examining the pictures and reading. Nodding her head, she looked up at the others in the room.

"We need to find this guy," she said.

"How can you say you don't believe in the power of dreams?" Alexa asked Ryan on the drive back to Boston. Kate and Lilith silently listened from the back seat.

"Oh, come on now, you're a rational person," Ryan retorted. "Dreams are made up of repressed memories, or things we've seen that sometimes we don't realize we've seen. They can be a mixture of TV shows that spark something from our lives."

"Are you implying only irrational people believe dreams can be based on events we haven't experienced?"

"Let's just review the facts," Ryan said, temporarily taking his eyes off the road to glance at Alexa. "Your Mom has this nightmare beginning in her teens. She sees three men in the dream. One of the men is her grandfather, who she visits from time to time. Kate, how often did you guys visit the O'Shea's?"

"From the time Lilith was a toddler, I took her over to the O'Shea's house at least once a year – usually during the holidays," Kate answered.

"So, until she was at least fourteen, she saw her grandfather every year."

"Right."

"Now Lilly," Ryan continued, "when did you start having the nightmares?"

"I think they started when I was around fifteen," she replied.

"So, your grandfather dies when you're fourteen. Even though you're not close to him, it could have been a traumatic experience. In all those visits to their house, don't you think you could have seen pictures of the family? After all, Dan O'Shea was quite the photographer."

"I guess I could have seen some of the family photos," Lilith admitted. "But I don't remember looking at any albums."

"Ahh," Ryan continued, "I'm thinking, judging by all the framed pictures around Mary's house, you at least saw some of those during your visits. I noticed several family photos from an earlier time with both Dan and Julia in them." Ryan paused for effect.

"And Lilly," he restarted, "weren't you good friends with Nick Jamison's granddaughter?"

"Well, we were friends in high school."

"Isn't it possible you saw pictures in her house of both Nick and Rosie in their younger days? And, weren't you around fifteen when you met Nick? And, didn't you say he gave you the creeps when you first met him? Perhaps that event, combined with delayed grieving for your grandfather triggered the nightmare." Ryan's cross-examination was getting on Alexa's nerves.

"You know," Alexa said, voice rising slightly, "you're nothing but a bully, poopy-face. You're picking on my Mom here."

"Poopy-face?" Ryan asked, a grin widening his cheeks.

"I'd call you something worse, except there are ladies in the back seat."

"Hey, don't hold back on our account," Kate said, smiling at her granddaughter's spunk.

"Okay," Alexa said, turning to face Ryan. "You're sounding like a complete asshole. This is not a courtroom, and my Mom is not a defendant. And, Mr. Know-it-all, you are not a lawyer. At least not until you finish law school." She sat back in her seat, and sighed.

"Now, let's look at some other facts," she said, regaining her composure. "Perhaps mom did see pictures of Dan and Nick when she was younger. But since there are only two pictures showing Tony, and chances are slim to none Mom ever saw them, how do you explain him being the third guy in her dream?"

Ryan opened his mouth to answer.

"I'm not done yet," Alexa said, cutting off any response. "Nana Kate, how old was Mom when you told her about Julia's murder?"

"She was eighteen," Kate replied. "I remember because we had just finished a visit with Mary, and Lilith overheard Mary saying how there was no doubt Lilith was Jack's daughter, and what a shame it was Julia's life was snuffed out before she could see Lilith. On the way home, Lilith started asking questions about why there would have been any question on who her father was, and how Julia died. I figured it was probably past the time when I should come clean, and told her everything."

"So," Alexa continued, "Mom didn't know about Julia's murder until she was eighteen. That's three years after she started having the nightmares. She couldn't have known about the lady floating in the river, or the significance of a scarf until she was eighteen. And," Alexa paused for dramatic effect, "she didn't know the identity of the third man until today. So there." She smiled triumphantly.

"I'm not conceding the identity of Nick and Dan," Ryan said. "And perhaps Lilly's dream developed or expanded as her brain absorbed other facts. Like maybe, this last one was more specific because she had looked at the case file. Perhaps her memory of the nightmare assumed it had always contained all the new details."

"That still doesn't explain Tony," Alexa said.

"Okay, I give," Ryan said, holding his hands over his head.

"Get your hands back on wheel, young man, before you kill us all," Lilith scolded.

CHAPTER 26

Frank sensed the tension between Alexa and Ryan as they stomped into the office, followed by Lilith and Kate.

"Did you guys have a lover's spat, or something?" he asked. Frank stopped his attempts at humor when Alexa's head whipped in his direction, hands on her hips in a defensive, angry stance. Ryan mumbled something indiscernible ending with the word "women", as he headed to his desk.

"They'll be okay," Kate said, approaching Frank's desk. "Just had a difference of opinion. Nothing that won't blow over." She sat in the side chair, propping her chin in her hand, elbow on his desk, looking directly at him, and then asked, "So, what have you been up to while we've been gone? Did you miss us?"

Frank cleared his throat. "I've actually made some headway in the case," he announced to the room in general.

"I thought you were going to wait until I got back," Alexa said, voiced edged in ice.

"Now don't get your panties in a twist. I just did a little bit of digging to find out where Eddie Jamison has gotten to. I went down to Human Resources. They show his pension check is divided between two bank accounts. Guess his ex got her hands on half of it. The address they have on file for him is in Somerville. We can head over there tomorrow."

"Well, okay then," Alexa relented. "Just so you didn't go off interviewing people without me." Her cell phone chimed, ending the conversation. Opening the phone, she was puzzled to hear the recently familiar voice of Colleen.

"Mary and I continued talking about Mom and everything after you guys left," she started. "And we came up with something you might want to check out."

"Mind if I put you on speaker, so everyone can hear?" Alexa asked.

"No problem." Everyone gathered around Alexa's phone.

"Anyway, as I was saying," Colleen shouted, "Mary and I thought of something after you left. Mom's birthday is coming

113

up in a few days. We always go to the cemetery to leave flowers in the morning, before going to mass. It's our way of remembering her. Tommy always went to the grave after work. Said there were other flowers by her tombstone."

"That's nice," Kate said, hand revolving in a silent pantomime to get the conversation moving. "But what's this got to do with the case? And you don't need to shout into the phone to be heard."

"Well, we don't know who it is that leaves the other flowers on her grave," Colleen continued, voice lowered. "One year, we went back right after mass to see if the other flowers were there. They were there alright. So, whoever brings them must do it while we're at mass. We never really thought anything of it. Just figured it was some friend. No big deal."

"What kind of flowers are they?" Ryan asked.

"They're always white roses. A dozen of them."

"Hmm, white roses," Lilith said. "Signifying innocence, or purity, or new beginnings. Wonder how they tie in."

"There's more," Colleen said, interrupting Lilith's musings. "Dad used to take flowers to the cemetery every year on the day Mom died. He told me there was always a bouquet of red roses and white carnations set on her grave before he got there. Really pissed him off. After Dad died, I took over the duty. Sure enough, the bouquet was always there. But then, about twenty years ago, it stopped. We never knew who put them there, or why they stopped."

"Well, thanks for the information," Alexa said. "If you think of anything else, please call me. We'll check out the cemetery to find out this mystery person."

Colleen gave Alexa the date, location of Julia's grave site, and morning mass time. Out of respect, Kate offered to attend mass with the sisters.

"That's a shocker," Alexa said to Kate. "You're passing up the chance to go on a stakeout to attend mass?"

"Stakeouts bore me," Kate replied.

"When were you ever on a stakeout to know they're boring?"

"There're things about me you don't need to know, my dear." Kate's eyebrows wriggled up and down.

CHAPTER 27

B efore heading out to Somerville the next day, everyone
decided Lilith should go on all interviews. Judging by
Colleen and Mary's reaction, her resemblance to Julia sparked
memories. Not to be left behind, Kate insisted that as historian
of the group, she needed to be included.

"So, what did you tell Eddie we were coming to see him
about?" Alexa asked Frank as they left the office.

"I told him I had an intern looking into an old case of his
for a school project."

"You didn't tell him which case it was, did you?"

"No, and he didn't ask. He just chuckled and said something like, 'Hey, anything to help out a fellow cop and his
underling.' I could almost picture his chest jutting out with
some warped sense of self-importance."

Crossing the Charles River, they drove along Monsignor
O'Brien Highway, past the Museum of Science, into
Somerville, located only two miles from Boston. As the most
densely populated city in New England, Somerville's houses
were set up in cemetery style – rows of closely-packed houses
along narrow one-way streets, with small abutting backyards
separated by chain link fences.

"Trivia time," Kate said from the back seat. "What is one of
Somerville's most well-known products?"

"Traffic," Frank grumbled as he wound through the streets.

"Nope."

"Well, it certainly isn't fine china or crystal," Lilith said.

"Nope."

"How about Irish lace curtains?" Alexa guessed.

"Not even close," Kate said. "It's marshmallow fluff."

"I like fluff and peanut butter sandwiches," Frank
responded, as they parked in front of a house broken up into
several apartments, paint peeling from its clapboards. "Maybe
Eddie will make us some for lunch."

Eddie Jamison met them at the front door, opening into a small one-bedroom apartment reeking of stale smoke and dirty laundry. In his early seventies, Eddie had not aged well. His stooped shoulders betrayed a once tall frame. Thinning gray hair outlined weathered skin, pug nose, weak chin, and small eyes constantly darting like balls from a pinball machine.

"Nice place, huh?" Eddie asked, looking at Frank. "You'd think one of Boston's finest could afford something better in retirement." His cackle turned into hacking. "But no. That damned cow I married gets half my pension." Another wet hack erupted from his lungs, which he visibly swallowed, prominent Adam's apple bobbing.

"Who'd you bring with you?" he asked, shifting his gaze to the three women. Before Frank could make introductions, Eddie moved closer to Lilith, squinting. He shook his head, eyes closed. Reopening his eyes, he glanced at Kate.

"Hey, you look familiar," he said to Kate. "Older, but familiar."

"I'm Kate Gallagher," she said, extending her hand. "I was a couple of years behind you in high school." Eddie ignored Kate's hand, moving closer to her. Recognition altered his features – raised eyebrows produced more wrinkles on his lined forehead. He grinned, showing tobacco-stained uneven teeth.

"You dated that whack-job, Jack O'Shea, didn't ya?" Eddie asked.

Kate's spine straightened, lips tightened as she resisted any retort that might antagonize him.

Looking back at Lilith, Eddie's face paled.

"My god," he whispered, "you look like Jack's Mom, come back from the dead." He hesitated, eyes moving up and down as he examined her. "Who the hell are you?"

"I'm Lilly," she stated firmly. "Daughter of Kate and Jack." Hand sweeping toward Alexa, Lilith continued, "And this is my daughter, Alexa." Eddie nodded slightly, and then his neck turned slowly, reptilian-like, to Kate.

"So you and Jack got hitched?" he asked.

Tempted to tell him the real story about Lilith's conception just to shock him, Kate decided to continue the tale fabricated by her mother.

"We picked up our friendship after college," Kate replied. "I went out to California to visit him one summer, and we discovered we were still in love. We decided to get married when he returned from Nam. Unfortunately, he was killed over there before he even learned I was pregnant."

"Well ain't that a sweet story," Eddie cackled. "So's your granddaughter here the police intern?"

"Yes, she is. Alexa's working on one of your old cases."

The cob webs clogging Eddie's brain parted. His hands started shaking. He stumbled over to a sagging chair, slowly releasing his weight into the well-worn cushion.

"You're here to talk about the Julia O'Shea case, ain't ya? I knew that damned case would come back to haunt me someday."

CHAPTER 28

"You always were perceptive," Frank said to Eddie, smirking slightly. "So, why don't you tell us what you remember."

Hesitantly, Kate, Lilith and Alexa lined up on the couch, half expecting their weight on the decrepit furniture to scatter roaches. Alexa pulled her notebook out of her oversized purse. Eddie lit a cigarette, inhaling deeply. The exhaled smoke swirled toward the ceiling, already yellowed from years of nicotine.

"I was having a late lunch with Uncle Nick," Eddie began. "I'd run into him the night before while I was on duty. Got a call about some domestic disturbance on Marlborough Street."

Lilith and Alexa exchanged glances. Could this be the same incident they read about in the library's microfiche?

"Why don't you tell us about the call-out first," Lilith suggested. Frank and Kate looked over at Lilith, eyebrows raised. Meeting their gazes, she shook her head to ward off any questions.

"Oh, it wasn't nothing much," Eddie said, waving his hand in the air. "Just some old biddies complaining about noises coming from one of the apartments. When I got there and knocked on the door, Uncle Nick answered. I remember I was surprised to see him, but then he reminded me he kept the place for special meetings. He winked at me so I'd get the drift." Eddie cackled.

"What do you mean by special meetings?" Alexa asked.

"He'd take his dolls up there. Usually picked 'em up at bars." Eddie chuckled, his pot belly gyrating.

"He was holding a towel to his head," he continued. "Had ice in it. Asked him if he needed any help. Said no – that he'd whacked his head on the bathroom floor when he slipped getting outta the shower. I told him about the complaints, and he said he had the TV up loud while he was in the bathroom. Said he'd been cussin' up a storm tryin' to get ice on his head before it swelled too much."

"Did you go inside the apartment?" Alexa asked.

"Didn't have to. We talked at the door. He said to offer his apologies to the nosy biddies for being so loud. He'd already turned the TV down. Asked if I could keep his name outta the papers. It'd be embarrassing for his kid, Missy. I was fine with that." Eddie paused, eyes moving to the ceiling. "In fact, we had to get going anyways. Got a call about some bar fight at Riley's Pub."

"Was anyone with Nick in the apartment?" Alexa asked. Eddie's eyes blinked like he was sending Morse code messages. Stubbing out his cigarette, he reached for the pack, and tapped out another butt. With unsteady hands, he flicked his lighter several times to ignite his cigarette.

"Naw, he was alone."

"How do you know, if you didn't go into the apartment?"

"Didn't hear no voices from inside." Eddie sat back, crossing his arms tight across his chest.

"So, you met Nick for lunch the next day," Frank prompted, switching the questions to focus Eddie on the day of the murder.

Eddie uncrossed his arms and leaned forward, bony elbows resting on bony knees.

"Yeah. I asked how his head was, and he said he had one helluva headache, but it was okay. I was headed back to my squad car when I heard the radio squawk. They was calling for anyone on duty near the Charles to get over there. So, I hopped in, turned on my siren, and headed to the river."

"How did you get the case?" Frank asked.

"My partner, Billy Deavers, was first senior guy on the scene. The diver was pushing the net over to the river bank when I got there. Pulled her up and laid her on the ground." Eddie paused, shaking his head. "I remember that god-awful scream from Jack. Poor kid." He hacked before continuing.

"Looking over at Jack, I remember seeing Uncle Nick up on the bridge. Don't know why he was there. Guess he heard my radio and was curious, just like the other lookers." Eddie's shoulders heaved in a shrug.

"What did you notice about the body when she was by the river?" Alexa asked.

"She wasn't bloated. But cold as a fish. She had on a dress and a scarf, but no undies. Billy pulled down her dress so her privates wouldn't show. He was decent like that. Didn't care if the coroners got pissed or not. The ambulance took her away so they could do the autopsy. Didn't give us much to go on, except she was strangled before being put in the river. Based the time of death on river tides. But I'm sure you've looked at their report. Probably give you more information than my memory."

"How'd the investigation go without much to go on?" Alexa asked.

"We talked to the old lady who reported the body in the river," Eddie responded. "But she didn't know nothing. Looked for tire marks or drag marks near where she was found. Again, nothing. Then, we looked up river for any signs she was put in somewheres else. Couldn't find nothing." Eddie shook his head, emphasizing his statement.

"Interviewed the family, but that led nowhere. Old man O'Shea just said she'd been gone for a few days. Didn't know where she'd gone. When we pressed him, he said she'd do that a few times every year. Just needed to get away from the kids to have time for herself. He'd go and pick her up at some diner, but they'd never talk about where she went." Eddie paused, shaking his head. "Don't seem right. What man lets his wife just go off without knowing where? But we couldn't crack him. Stubborn coot. The kids were too young to be any help. And Jack ... well, he just wasn't talking to no one. Interviewed some neighbors, but they didn't help with much information." Eddie lit another cigarette. Blowing out the smoke through his nose, he lifted his index finger.

"Wait a minute. I remember we interviewed Greg Lyons. He worked with Dan. Told us he'd gone to see Dan that night. Something about having seen Julia in town at some bar, cavorting with a man." Eddie chuckled. "Guess Dan got pretty mad 'cause he'd thrown Greg outta his house."

"Did Greg tell you who was with Julia?" Alexa asked.

"Don't think so," Eddie said, looking down at the ashtray, tapping his cigarette several times. Alexa glanced at Ryan, eyebrows raised.

"Are you sure?" Alexa persisted.

"Look, I said I don't remember," Eddie spat, crossing his arms across his chest.

"Okay then," Frank said. "What else do you remember?"

"Do remember talking to Nick about the case," Eddie continued, blowing smoke at the ceiling. "Went over to his house for dinner one night. Wanted to run things by him. He was a smart fella – a natural investigator with his work in insurance. Rosie came outta the kitchen and said Julia was probably running around with men when she took off. Said she was a real tramp. I remember Nick yelling at her to shut up. Said she didn't know what she was talking about. You know the history of Rosie and Julia and Nick, don't ya?" Everyone nodded. "Well, that's why I never put any credence into what Rosie said. Figured it was just her jealousy talking. She's still a crazy old bat."

"She's still alive?" Kate asked.

"Yeah. Moved in with Missy after Nick died. Must be about twenty years ago. She and Missy'd sit in the kitchen guzzling beer for hours on end, bad-mouthing men. I'd run into Bobby – that's Missy's husband – at some bar, and he'd tell me what bitches they both were. Felt sorry for Missy's kids. Few years back, I guess Bobby had enough of it. Insisted they put Rosie in a home down in Quincy. She's gotta be in her nineties now. Guess it's true what they say. Only the good die young. Figure the devil and God keep arguing about who has to take her, so they just leave her here." Eddie chuckled at his own joke.

"Is there anything else you can tell us about Julia's murder?" Alexa asked.

"Nothing I remember," he said, shaking his head. "Really hope you figure it out. Nick told me she was a good woman. Didn't deserve being killed. Told me over drinks about a year before he died that Julia was the only woman he ever really loved. Only time I felt sorry for the guy."

Frank thanked Eddie as they left, telling him to call if he remembered anything else about the case.

"Ewww," Lilith said, shivering, as they got in the car. "I feel like I have cooties now."

"So why'd you have Eddie tell us about the domestic disturbance incident?" Frank asked Alexa.

"It was in an article Mom and I found at the library," she said. "I don't know whether there's any connection, or not. But it just seems so strange how Nick keeps popping up all over the case. Too bad he's dead, or we could talk to him to see what he knew about Julia. Maybe we should see if we can interview Rosie."

"She's probably senile," Frank said. "I don't know if we could trust her memory."

"Maybe she's not as crazy as everyone thinks," Alexa retorted.

CHAPTER 29

"Hi, hon," Bill greeted Lilith the next evening, entering their kitchen while she was rinsing carrots and green beans for dinner. "You know," he continued, "I really like your hair in curls. Rather sexy." She chuckled as he buried his nose in her hair, running his hands down her spine, stopping at her ass. He pulled her close to him.

"Yeah," she whispered, "I may just keep it this way." Their lips met, softly caressing – a promise of coming passion. Lilith felt the longing travel down Bill's torso, hardening against her. She moaned softly as their kiss matched the tempo of their desire.

"Whoopsie," Kate said, entering the kitchen, then turning, shielding her eyes. "You guys really should get a room. You'll wilt the veggies with all that steam."

Lilith jumped out of Bill's embrace, while he slowly turned to the sink, grasping the twin bowls, head lowered.

"Why don't you just dump cold water down my pants," he mumbled. Turning his face toward Lilith, he winked, suggesting they would pick up where they left off later in the evening.

"Kate, your timing is unbelievable," Lilith scolded, smiling at Bill.

"Hey, better I find you than one of the kids. You could scar them for life. By the way, did you remember you invited Ryan and Frank for dinner?"

"Of course, I remembered. That's why there are seven steaks on the platter."

Bill stepped over to the liquor cabinet, pulling out the scotch and vodka, along with three glasses. He needed a stiff drink, and figured Lilith could use one too. Kate was always ready for at least one before-dinner drink.

"So, what's the next step in Alexa's case?" he asked, dropping ice cubes into the glasses. He poured the scotch in two glasses, added filtered water from the refrigerator, then fixed Lilith's vodka and tonic.

"Tomorrow morning we're going over to the cemetery to see if we can find out who leaves flowers on Julia's grave every year," Lilith replied, taking a sip from her drink.

"You're going on a stakeout?" Bill asked. "Better be prepared to sit for awhile. Those things can take hours."

"I'll probably take a book along."

Alexa entered the kitchen through the back door, followed by Ryan and Frank.

"We're home," she announced before turning to Lilith. "You look flushed, Mom. Are you feeling okay?"

"I'm fine, honey. Just a bit warm in the kitchen."

Kate laughed and closed her mouth with a smile as Lilith shot her a warning glance. Bill coughed to disguise his chuckle. Alexa shrugged, not really wanting to know the source of their mirth.

"So, what can I get you fellas to drink?" Bill asked after introductions were made.

"Got any beer?" Frank asked. Bill handed him a cold beer and iced mug from the freezer.

"I'll have an iced tea, if you have any," Ryan replied.

"Hey, you're not on duty," Kate said. "You can have something stronger, if you want." She paused, eyes drifting to the ceiling before settling back on his face. "Oh, or did you mean a Long Island iced tea? I don't know if we have all the makings for one of those."

"No, just regular iced tea is fine."

Kate shrugged as Bill handed Ryan a tall glass of tea.

"Why don't you guys help me with the grill," Bill suggested, picking up the platter before heading outside. Frank and Ryan followed.

"Where's Johnny?" Alexa asked.

"We just finished our jam session," Kate replied. "He's already outside, waiting to help with the grilling. He was excited to meet your partners. I expect he'll be peppering them with questions about now."

"I do hope he won't make a pest of himself," Alexa said, as she headed to the dining room with plates and flatware.

"That was a fine meal, Lilly" Frank said, patting his stomach after the main course was completed. "I must say that I feel more like I do now than I did when I came in." He chuckled as everyone looked at him, perplexed.

"Uh, thanks," Lilith said, not sure how to take his compliment.

"So, what's the plan for tomorrow?" Kate asked.

"Mass is at nine o'clock," Ryan said. "The sisters said they always go to Julia's grave before mass, and the anonymous flowers aren't there. So, we should get to the cemetery just before they leave for church. Mass is over at about ten. Our guy must put them there during that hour."

"But he may be there before nine," Frank added. "May watch the sisters leave before going to the grave. So let's get there by eight."

"I'm joining Colleen and Mary for Mass," Kate said. "To keep up appearances, I should probably meet them somewhere and go in their car. I'll call them to arrange a meeting place. But I'll keep my eyes open at the cemetery."

"Just don't be too conspicuous," Alexa warned. "We don't want to spook this guy."

"Hey, I'm not spooky," Kate retorted. "I can be subtle."

Alexa rolled her eyes.

"The rest of us will meet at the station," Ryan said. "We'll take two cars, so we don't look suspicious. And we'll set up in different spots. Alexa will go with me, and Lilly will ride with Frank."

"I'm driving," Alexa said, chin thrust forward indignantly.

Bill looked at Ryan, imperceptibly shaking his head – a warning not to argue with her.

CHAPTER **30**

Two cars headed to Saint Timothy's. Adjacent to the church, the cemetery sat atop a small knoll, its drive winding around avenues of tombstones. Dates on the markers ranged from the early nineteenth century to current times. Large oak and maple trees sat amid tributes both large and ornate to mere stones in the ground, etched with names and remembrances of the dead.

"According to Colleen," Alexa said, eyes roaming the cemetery before focusing on one spot. "Julia's gravesite is over there – the fourth one past that tree."

"Let's drive up to the top of the hill," Ryan said. "It'll give us a good vantage point." After parking several rows up the hill, they sat in the car under the shade of an oak, watching.

Meanwhile, Frank and Lilith parked two avenues to the side of the designated site. The sun was quickly warming the outside temperature, heralding another mid-summer dog day. Frank opened both windows, allowing a faint breeze into the car.

"Shouldn't we get out of the car, as if we're here to visit someone?" Lilith asked. "I brought these flowers from my garden to make us look authentic." She lifted the bouquet of pale purple irises and white baby's breath from her lap. "We look rather stupid sitting here with flowers."

"You're probably right," Frank admitted. "Ryan and Alexa can get away with just sitting in the car." He chuckled. "If they sit close enough, people might think they're just here to make out. But we're too old for that." He grinned, wriggling his bushy eyebrows, while rotating the toothpick dangling from his mouth.

"Hey, I'm a married woman."

"All the more reason you'd be out here to carry on an illicit affair." He was enjoying making her squirm a bit.

"Just keep your hands to yourself," Lilith said, voice rising an octave.

"Relax, Lilly. Just kidding. Besides, you're not my type. Too skinny."

"I don't know whether to be flattered or insulted," she said, sighing. "Why do I always fall for pranks?"

"Gullible," Frank said flatly.

"Am not."

"Are too."

Lilith felt the giggle bubble in her stomach, tickling her ribs, before it escaped. Frank snorted his hearty laugh.

A white Jaguar entered through the gates. As the car climbed the hill, the four observers noticed its classic design. The man driving sat on the right side, signifying the car's origin as England. The car wandered to the opposite end of the cemetery.

"Think that's him?" Alexa asked Ryan, from their location.

"Hard to tell. He's disappeared over that ridge."

"Here come Nana Kate and the sisters," she said, pointing toward a mini-van entering the winding drive.

As the women parked and exited the vehicle, Kate looked up at Alexa's car, rubbing her finger across the side of her nose.

"Oh god," Alexa moaned, "she thinks she's in that movie, *The Sting*. Next thing you know, she'll expect Paul Newman or Robert Redford to appear."

"I get to be Redford," Ryan said. "Frank can be Newman."

"This isn't funny," Alexa snapped. "She could blow this whole thing." She paused, closing her eyes, hands steepled. "Please, please, Nana Kate, don't do anything else." She opened her eyes, staring at the three women.

Colleen and Mary slowly knelt in front of the stone, gently placing a bouquet of yellow daylilies, pink roses and white carnations on the ground. Kate remained standing, head turning as her eyes wandered around the cemetery, settling on the grave next to where the sisters knelt. Her hand jerked to her mouth, as if stifling a sob. Colleen said something to Kate, slightly tugging on her hem. Kate joined the sisters, kneeling, bowing her head. Then Kate took a single rose from the bouquet, placing it on the next grave. A few moments passed before the three women rose to their feet, brushing their knees. They strolled to the mini-van, got in, and drove back down the hill toward the church.

"What was that about?" Frank asked.

"I think the grave next to Julia's is Jack's," Lilith replied. "Never thought about that possibility when she volunteered to accompany the sisters." Lilith paused, shaking her head. "Must have been hard for her."

"Well, it should be time for our guy to show," Frank said after clearing his throat.

"I'm gonna get out and wander around a bit," Lilith said, opening the car door, carrying her flowers. "I'll go to some grave site, lay down the flowers, and then walk around as if meditating."

"Maybe you could throw in a few sobs," Frank suggested.

As Lilith headed to the row of grave stones in front of Julia's, an elderly man strode down the lane and turned at Julia's row. His thick stock of white hair topped a slightly weathered face. Erect back and shoulders of his average build contrasted bowed legs and splayed feet, akin to Charlie Chaplin. He was dressed in a dark blue suit, a cravat in place of a tie.

"Where the hell did he come from?" Frank's attention had been focused on Lilith. Looking out his side window, he noticed the white Jaguar several yards away. Ryan and Alexa had exited their car and were slowly strolling down the hill.

The man bent arthritic knees, lowering himself while clutching onto Julia's headstone. He placed a dozen white roses next to the flowers Colleen and Mary left. Lilith walked toward the grave. Sunlight filtering through limbs of an oak tree back-lighted her silhouette. Moving forward, her shadow fell across the stone. The man looked up, squinting against the sunlight. His features softened as he grasped the headstone and started to rise.

"J-Julia?" he stuttered.

Before Lilith could respond, he stood quickly, defying his arthritic knees, lurched forward and embraced her tightly, sobbing into her hair. The pounding of her heart at the sudden movement caught a scream in her throat. She relaxed as she heard the man repeating Julia's name.

Witnessing the scene, Alexa and Ryan ran down the hill. Lilith held up her hand behind the man's back to ward them off. She knew he meant her no harm. She held him, gently stroking his back to calm his sobs. Her flowers dropped on Julia's grave.

Suddenly, the man's torso tightened and straightened. His arms dropped to his sides as he stepped back.

"You can't be Julia," he whispered, head lowered, shaking from side to side. "She's been dead for fifty years." He looked up at Lilith before asking, "Who the hell are you?"

"I'm Julia's granddaughter, Lilly." As Lilith stared at this stranger, trying to erase fifty years from his face, imaginary fingers snapped in her head. He might be the third man from her dream.

CHAPTER 31

Alexa, Ryan and Frank sauntered over to Lilith and the stranger. Taking his eyes off Lilith, the stranger's gaze roamed to each of the three newcomers.

"Who are you people?" he asked, bewildered. He shifted his weight, as if ready to run.

"They're with me," Lilith replied calmly. "You're Tony Bronkowski, aren't you?"

"Y-yes, I am," the man stuttered. "B-but how do you know who I am? I'm not doing anything wrong by being here. Just paying my respects to an old friend." The lines on his weathered face smoothed as he looked down at Julia's grave.

"I'll get right to the point, Mr. Bronkowski," Lilith said.

"Tony's okay," he said.

"Okay then, Tony. As I said, I'm Lilly, Julia's granddaughter. This," she said, motioning with a sweep of her arm, "is Alexa, my daughter. And these gentlemen are Ryan and Frank." The men shook hands with Tony.

"I can understand why you and your daughter are here to pay respects," Tony said, leaning into Lilith, conspiratorially, jerking his thumb toward Ryan and Frank . "But why are these guys here?"

"They're police officers."

"But I'm not doing anything wrong," Tony protested.

"No, you're not," Frank said. "We're here looking into who killed Julia."

Tony's hands involuntarily clasped in the middle of his chest, as he sucked in his breath. His face paled before his eyes disappeared behind their lids. His body slackened, folding at odd angles around his waist and knees. Ryan rushed to catch Tony, as he began his descent to the ground. Ryan felt Tony's neck, checking his pulse, and nodded to the others.

"You big lout," Lilith snapped at Frank, swatting his arm. "You didn't have to be so damned blunt. You could've killed him." She paused, glaring at Frank. "There's some water in your car. Go get it."

Frank wasn't accustomed to obeying orders from a civilian. Hell, it's why he was divorced – twice. But he also knew when to pick battles and wars. This one wasn't worth fighting over. He jogged to the car, retrieved two bottles of water, then walked briskly back to the others. Lilith was on the ground, Tony's head in her lap. Frank handed her a bottle of water.

"Here, drink this," Lilith whispered as Tony's eyes fluttered open. Sipping the water, Tony started to speak.

"Shhh for now," Lilith said. "Let's get you over to that bench in the shade … then we'll talk." With Ryan's help, Tony stood, walked slowly to the bench and sat down. Lilith sat next to him, while the others stood nearby.

"Alexa has a summer job with the police," Lilith started. "As a school project, she wanted to look into an unsolved case. My mother, Kate, suggested she look into Julia's death."

"What's this Kate have to do with Julia?" Tony asked, brow wrinkled.

"Kate dated Julia's son, Jack, in high school, at the time when Julia was killed." Lilith sighed before continuing. "As you may have guessed, Jack was my father."

"Oh dear," Tony said, patting Lilith's hands. "I read about Jack being killed in Nam. So sorry."

"Thank you. I never knew him. He died before I was born." Lilith's eyes were drawn to the ground by movement. Frank was tapping his foot. She looked up, glaring, lips tightened. His foot stopped.

"So, none of this speaks to how you know who I am," Tony said.

"We saw an old picture of you playing the piano, with Julia singing," Alexa interjected. "Her husband, Dan, wrote your name on the back of the picture."

"Ahh, Dan," Tony said, nodding his head. "Helluva good man. Must have been at Jack's birthday."

"So, how did you know Julia?" Alexa asked.

"That's a long story," Tony replied. His smile erased more lines than it created.

"We've got nothing but time," Alexa said as she lowered herself to the ground in front of Tony like a young child anticipating her grandfather's latest tale. Frank and Ryan remained standing, shifting their weight in readiness.

"I was twenty-one when I met Julia," Tony started, eyes twinkling. "Somewhere around nineteen fifty or fifty-one. She came into the bar where I worked – called The Club. After a shift of making drinks, I'd sit at the piano and take requests. She sat down by the piano and asked me to play 'Don't Fence Me In'. Never forget it. Prettiest gal I'd ever seen. Lose yourself in those eyes. Voice like a lark. Sure, she was older than me. Didn't matter. We were like best friends ... at least until he'd arrive." Tony paused, a frown replacing lost wrinkles. He sighed, straightening his shoulders before continuing.

"Julia would have everyone singing along. Real life of the party, she was. She'd come in like that for three or four nights in a row. Then she'd come in and ask me to play something sad, like 'I'll Be Seeing You' or 'Unforgettable'. Go on like that 'til closing time. Whenever I'd play something upbeat, she'd go sit in the corner. At the end of those nights, she'd come and ask if she could stay with me. We'd go back to my place. Nothing ever happened. I'd just hold her while she cried herself to sleep. Next morning I'd walk her to Joe's Diner. I'd call Dan to come pick her up. Sat with her 'til he got there. He never asked me any questions. Just thanked me for staying with her. Then he'd wrap his arms around her, they'd walk to his car and drive off." Tony's shoulders slumped, shaking. Tears trickled down his weathered cheeks.

"How often did she come around?" Alexa asked.

"Three, maybe four times a year." Tony sniffed, wiping away his tears with the back of his hand, spotted with age.

"Was it at any particular time every year?"

"Nope. Never knew when she'd pop in. I worked at that bar real steady back then. Folks liked me. I was rather good at the piano, if I do say so myself."

"Do you know whether she went to any other places?"

"Nope," Tony replied, shaking his head. "Said I was her favorite accompanist." The broad smile returned.

"So, where would she go on the nights she didn't leave with you?" Alexa asked. Tony's smile disappeared.

"I usually don't like speaking ill of the dead," he began, "but that son-of-a-bitch just wasn't good for her. Tried telling her so one time. Nearly bit my head off, telling me it wasn't any of my business."

"So, who was it?" Alexa persisted.

"That damned Nick Jamison," Tony replied.

CHAPTER 32

L ilith and Alexa's heads whipped to exchange glances. Then they looked at Ryan and Frank. The foursome's eyebrows arched like the cables on the Zakim Bridge. Noticing the movement, Tony's glance roved about his audience.

"You guys know Nick?" Tony asked.

"Met him a few times," Frank answered. "Didn't really know him as much as knew about him."

"I was friends with his granddaughter in high school," Lilith said. "I saw him at her house. Didn't talk to him very often. He was quiet then. Just sat in the living room watching TV."

"Well, if you looked anything then like you do now," Tony said, chuckling, "I'll bet you gave him a start when he saw you. Especially those eyes. Just like Julia's."

"So, what can you tell us about Nick?" Alexa asked.

"He was a regular at The Club," Tony said. "Had his usual table off in the corner. He'd come in, looking quite dapper in an expensive suit, hair slicked down. Usually had some babe on his arm. Never the same one twice. Good lookers though. Sometimes he'd come in alone, and pick up someone before long. Go over to his corner table, and get real cozy with the broad. Never left alone. Spent a fortune. Good tipper." Tony pulled a handkerchief from his pocket, dabbing at his forehead before continuing.

"The first night I met Julia, Nick was in there alone. When she started singing, he moved to a table right up front. She gave him a little finger wave while she was singing. After that first song, she went over to him and gave him a big hug. Like they were old friends or something. She left with him at closing time. Every time she came into The Club, he'd be there. Always sat up front. She'd leave with him – except the last nights when she'd go home with me."

"Do you know where they went?" Alexa asked.

"Heard Nick had some apartment near The Club where he'd take his ladies. Don't know exactly where it was. Always assumed that's where they'd go." Tony lowered and shook his head. "Couldn't understand it. I know Julia loved Dan. Said so to me plenty of times. Yet she'd go cavorting with Nick. Asked her about it one time. She said they were friends from the old days, when she used to perform in Scollay Square. Wouldn't tell me anything else. Just smiled that sweet smile of hers. Always melted my heart."

"Did Julia leave The Club with Nick the night she was murdered?" Ryan asked.

"Yeah, she did," Tony whispered. His gaze wandered over to Julia's grave, shoulders slumped.

"Do you remember what time they left?"

"Yeah," Tony replied, bringing his attention back to Ryan. "Never forget that night. Julia had been back, singing at The Club, for a couple of nights. When she came in that night, Nick was with her, giggling like teenagers. Sat at the corner table rather than up front. She asked me to play 'Kisses Sweeter than Wine'. Kept looking over at Nick and blowing him kisses while she was singing. They were real lovey-dovey. Left early. About nine. She threw me a kiss as they were leaving, then winked." Tony sighed.

"Do you remember what she was wearing?" Alexa asked.

"A lovely flowered dress. Kind of loose and flowing. But still showed off her figure. She had a great figure. Curves in all the right places. Wore a scarf around her neck. Had on real nice dangling earrings. Some blue stones with diamonds around them. Nearly matched her eyes. Doubt if Dan could afford them. Probably Nick gave them to her." Tony sat forward, elbows propped on his knees, face buried in his hands. His shoulders heaved as quiet sobs escaped through his hands. Lilith rubbed his back, trying to soothe his tears.

Car doors slammed, startling Alexa. She turned to the sound and saw Kate, Colleen and Mary walking in their direction. Kate's shadow blocked the sun in front of Tony. Slowly, his face emerged from his hands as he looked up at her. She squatted, looking into his eyes.

"Hi there, I'm Kate. Are you our mystery flower man?"

"Name's Tony. Tony Bronkowski." He wiped tears from his eyes. His head cocked slightly as his left eyebrow raised in question.

"You Lilly's Mom?" Tony asked.

"Yes, I am."

"So, you were married to Julia's boy, Jack? Sad thing about him being killed in Nam. She was so proud of him. Told me how smart and athletic he was. Are you the one who put the flower on his grave over there?" Tony pointed toward the twin graves.

"Yes, I did," Kate answered softly. "But Jack and I didn't get a chance to get married before he died. The most precious gift he gave me was Lilith. She's our love child."

Lilith looked at Kate, eyes moistening. She had never heard Kate refer to her in those terms.

"Are these ladies Julia's girls?" Tony asked, straightening his arthritic knees to stand, and then moving toward Colleen and Mary. "Your Mom was proud of you girls, too. Said she loved you so much it hurt sometimes."

"How'd you know Mom?" Colleen asked.

"Played piano for her," Tony replied. "Remember me coming to your house one year for Jack's birthday? We were a regular duo back in the day. Entertained at parties together."

Lilith knew he was lying to save them grief. She guessed he was right. The truth would hurt. They didn't deserve that.

"So, that's why you bring her flowers on her birthday?" Mary asked.

"She was such a lovely woman. Made me laugh. Loved her like the older sister I never had. Just wanted to pay my respects without interrupting your time with her."

"Do you also bring flowers every year on the day of her death?" Kate asked.

"No, never did that," Tony replied. "Her birthday's special, not her death."

The sisters moved forward as one, arms wrapping around their mother's old friend. Tony put his arms around their waists, accepting their embrace.

"You want to get a sandwich, or something?" Colleen asked, backing away. "We'd really like to hear stories about Mom. There's a diner down the street."

"Sounds lovely," Tony replied. "I believe I'm finished talking with these folks." He looked over at Alexa. She nodded.

"Before you leave," Lilith said, looking through her purse, "will you give us your phone number, in case we want to reach you?" She handed him a piece of paper and pen. Tony jotted a number on the paper and returned it to her. "It's been a pleasure, Tony," Lilith said, as he strolled to his car.

"What'd I miss?" Kate asked after Tony left.

"Hey, you're the one who didn't want to go on a stakeout. Remember?" Alexa said, heading to her car in long strides. Kate followed, wobbling on her mid-heeled shoes through the grass.

"Hey, it's not nice to leave your Nana in the dark, you know. You were raised better than that." Alexa continued walking, her back to Kate.

"Awww, come on," Kate protested, arms spread.

Alexa opened the driver's door, turning to Kate. Her face lifted, eyes crinkled, as laughter erupted.

"Well, come on and get in," Alexa beckoned. "We'll go over everything back at the station."

"So Tony's the third guy from Lilith's dream?" Kate asked from the back seat.

"Looks that way," Alexa responded.

"Please, ladies, let's not talk about dreams again," Ryan begged.

"Oops, right," Kate said. "Don't want to start that up again." She stifled a giggle. "Well, what'd he say about Julia and the murder?"

"Here," Alexa said, tossing her notebook to the back seat, "you can look over my notes on the drive back. But let's wait 'til we're all together to get into any discussion." While Alexa concentrated on maneuvering her car through traffic, Kate read the notes. Ryan sat silently, occasionally gripping the dashboard as Alexa accelerated through yellow lights.

Back at the office, everyone settled into chairs, Frank comfortably leaning back, feet propped up on his desk, a new toothpick rotating in his mouth. Alexa opened her notebook. Lilith grabbed paper and pen, ready to be the designated recorder of their discussion. Scanning her notes, Alexa recapped the interview with Tony.

"Something's just not adding up," Alexa said, head tilted in her hand.

"Let's jot down the problem," Lilith suggested, pen poised in her fingers.

"Well," Alexa started, "Tony said Julia left The Club early the night before her body was found. She and Nick departed at around nine o'clock." Alexa flipped back to her notes of the interview with Eddie. "Now, Eddie said when he went on the domestic disturbance call, Nick was alone in the apartment. But I think he was lying."

"What makes you think that?" Frank asked.

"I was watching his body language when he answered the question about whether anyone else was there. Remember? His eyes were shiftier than usual, and he was blinking so much

I thought he was going into convulsions. Plus, he kept fidgeting with his cigarette pack and lighter. Then, he shut down any further discussion when he crossed his arms. He relaxed again once you shifted the questions back to the next day. I just know he's hiding something." Alexa tapped her pen on the notebook.

"He also lied about Greg Lyons," she continued. "The interview report clearly states Greg told them he saw Julia with Nick, and told Dan. I don't think it was just a memory lapse."

"So, either Eddie's lying, or Tony is," Lilith said.

"My vote's on Eddie," Kate chimed in, raising her hand. "He is a wretched little character, isn't he?"

"Too bad Eddie's old partner is dead," Frank said. "He was a good cop. Woulda told us the truth."

"Think we can get a copy of their report from that night?" Alexa asked.

"A fifty-year-old domestic disturbance that's not unsolved?" Frank responded, shaking his head. "Those files woulda been purged years ago."

"At the very least," Alexa said, "we should re-interview both Eddie and Tony."

"Wait a minute," Ryan inserted, waving his hands. "Let's make sure we're not jumping to conclusions, or making assumptions here. Maybe neither one of them is lying." Alexa glanced at Frank. He winked and nodded. She recalled his warning about making assumptions and smiled.

"What do you mean?" Alexa asked, looking back at Ryan, left eyebrow cocked.

"Maybe Julia left with Nick at nine o'clock, like Tony said. But rather than going to Nick's apartment, perhaps she decided to go someplace else."

"But where would she go?"

"Ever think she might have decided to go home?"

"Why would she do that?" Alexa asked. "Tony said she and Nick were all lovey-dovey when they left The Club. You think she changed her mind about being with him?"

"Well, she did have her mood swings." Ryan sat back, arms folded.

"You know," Kate said, "we never did ask Colleen and Mary about that day. We should probably talk to them, too."

"Can we have Eddie come in here?" Lilith asked, a quiver running through her body. "I really don't want to go back to that flea-trap of an apartment."

"It's better to have all of them come in here anyway," Ryan said. "We can control things better from our home turf."

Alexa started twisting the ends of her hair, deep in thought. Her instincts were guiding her in one direction, but the facts weren't following. And they still lacked the primary ingredient – motive.

"Let's line up suspects and motive," Alexa suggested.

Lilith grabbed a new piece of paper.

"I'd say, with what we know, Nick is the primary suspect," Alexa continued. "He was the last person seen with Julia. He had an apartment in Boston where he took women. Chances are pretty good he and Julia went there whenever she was in town. But what was his motive? According to Eddie, Nick loved her. Why would he kill her if they had been carrying on this affair for years?"

"All we know for certain," Ryan interjected, "is Tony saw them leave The Club together. We don't know what happened after that. Maybe she switched into one of her depressions and decided she wanted to go home. So, they fought. He was ready for some passion, and she cut him off mid-stream, so to speak."

"Hmm. Strangulation is normally a crime of passion, rather than pre-meditation. But would he be so angry with her that he'd kill her? He had to know she had these mood swings, having known her for all those years. Plus, Tony said Julia'd always spent the night with him when she'd get sullen. From the sounds of it, she was still in a manic period when she was with Nick that night. Could she have turned suddenly, like that?" Alexa snapped her fingers for emphasis.

"Okay then," Ryan said, "let's consider another scenario. After leaving The Club, she switches off after they get to Nick's place and have sex. She decides to go home, by cab, late at night. Dan isn't prepared for this change in her schedule. She reeks of sex when she comes in. He's finally had enough of her running around. In a fit of rage, he strangles her, drives her body back into Boston, and dumps it in the Charles."

"So, what you're saying," Alexa mused, her fingers steepled in front of her on the desk, "we have two suspects – Nick and

Dan." Alexa tapped her fingers against her mouth. "I know Dan had a temper. But he adored Julia. I just can't see him flipping out to that extent. Plus, wouldn't the kids have heard an argument?"

"Something we need to ask the sisters," Ryan said bluntly.

Frank watched the exchange between Alexa and Ryan, without interruption. They were good together, bouncing ideas back and forth without emotion. They'd make good partners someday.

"I'm still troubled by how much each of these guys loved Julia," Alexa said. "It takes time to strangle someone. Even if one of them was temporarily angry with her, I think he'd snap out of it during the act. Whoever did this had to look at her face while they were snuffing the life out of it." She began tapping the pencil on the desk. "And there's the clothing issue. She was found with only the dress and scarf. So, chances are, she was naked when she was strangled. Then, the killer put her dress back on before putting her in the river." She stopped, slowly shaking her head. "It just doesn't add up. We're missing something."

"Let's set up those second interviews," Ryan suggested. "There's more to be told than we've heard."

CHAPTER **34**

K ate called the sisters to set up the first interview, luring them with lunch afterwards. Lilith reached out to Tony, promising him an adventure on a Duck Boat when the follow-up questions ended. Everyone agreed Eddie should be interviewed last. Frank set it up.

"Well, we've got to be going," Lilith announced after all calls were made. "I have a family to feed. Come on Kate. Let's beat traffic. Will you be joining us, Alexa?"

"I need to stay here awhile to formulate the questions. I'll just grab something later."

"I've been neglecting other cases," Frank said, rising from his chair. "Need to do some follow-up on them." Turning to Lilith and Kate, he continued, "Ladies, I'll escort you out."

Ryan pulled up a chair at Alexa's work table, sitting precariously close to her.

"Okay," he said, "let's see what we have here." He leaned into her, looking at the notes spread on the table. Receiving no response from her, his eyes roamed to her face.

Staring into his eyes, Alexa felt a tingle flutter in her stomach. Her throat felt like she had swallowed sand. All she could manage was a weak smile, returned by his broad grin. He winked to break the tension.

"Um, let's start with the sisters," Alexa muttered, shifting her gaze down while shuffling through her notes.

For the next two hours they combed through all the paperwork to develop questions needing answers. Alexa set up separate documents on her laptop for the three interviews. Occasionally, Ryan paced the room while she typed.

When they got to the information needed from Eddie, he leaned over her shoulder, his cheek brushing her hair, as he glanced down at the screen.

Minty fresh. How does he keep his breath so minty fresh? The scent was mixed with the fragrance of her favorite aftershave.

Blinking to clear her thoughts, she realized the typo just as he mentioned it.

"I think you meant to type 'Nick', not 'Ryan'," he chuckled.

Feeling the heat rise up her neck, she corrected the error.

"I need a break," she announced, pushing back her chair. He quickly dodged the wheels aimed at his foot. While he continued to look at the screen, Alexa headed to the coffee pot. Leaning on the table, Ryan looked over his shoulder, admiring the naturally seductive swing of her hips. He smiled, knowing she wasn't aware of the lure held in her walk. No bounce or strut – just a gentle sway with each step, her long hair swinging in tempo. He backed up as she returned with her steaming cup.

Pursing her lips, she blew over the rim of the cup like she was aiming a kiss in his direction.

Finishing the interview questions, Alexa printed two copies. They silently read through the documents.

"Let's be sure we don't make any preconceived assumptions," Ryan said.

"One thing from talking to Tony still bothers me," Alexa said.

"What's that?"

"The flowers left on her grave on the anniversary of her death."

"Look back at your notes from when the sisters called us," Ryan suggested. Alexa fingered back through her documents.

"Says the flowers stopped about twenty years ago," she said.

"And when did Nick die?" Ryan prompted.

"Same timeframe." Alexa looked at Ryan, sitting a whisper away. Another heart flutter. She quietly cleared her throat before continuing. "So, I guess we can assume he was the bearer." Ryan nodded, smiling.

For the next hour Alexa and Ryan amended the questions.

Ryan stretched his tall frame, back arched, hands rubbing his lower back, while Alexa turned off the laptop.

"What say we grab a bite to eat?" Ryan suggested. "There's a pub a couple of blocks away. My treat."

"Okay," Alexa responded. "My stomach's starting to purr."

"Purr?"

"Yeah. Men's stomachs growl. Women's purr."

His head tilted back as a hearty laugh escaped and tears formed in his eyes. The laugh was infectious. Alexa bent forward, holding her stomach as convulsions rippled through her.

"I think we're punch drunk," she said, wiping her own tears.

Careful not to discuss the case in public, they explored mutual interests while they ate.

"Didn't take you for someone who would skydive," Ryan said, finishing his sandwich. "Exhilarating, isn't it?"

"Yeah," Alexa said, "preceded by abject terror. The only way I went through with it was that I was first out of the plane. If I'd had to watch others disappear into the sky, I may have chickened out. But since I was bound tightly to the real jumper, that choice wasn't really mine."

"Would you do it again?" Ryan asked.

"Probably. But next time I'd keep my mouth closed. My throat was dry as dirt by the time we landed."

After dinner, Ryan walked Alexa to her car. She clicked the door unlocked and he started to walk away. But just as she reached to open the door, Ryan pivoted. Long strides brought him to her. He reached one arm around her waist, pulling her close to him. Her face tilted up to his, eyes at half-mast. She gasped, and then fully accepted his open kiss. She moaned softly as his hands gently explored her body. Their tongues flickered in greeting. Leaning into him closer, she felt his excitement.

Suddenly, the beep of another car being unlocked echoed through the lot. Startled, Alexa pulled away. The shaking of her hands kept tempo with her heart beat.

"Umm, I guess I better be going," she whispered.

"You okay?" he asked, concern replacing passion in his expression.

"Yeah," she sighed, nodding her head, eyes mirroring the slight smile dancing on her lips. "Couldn't be better."

"We'll continue this later," Ryan said, his trademark smile assuring future encounters.

CHAPTER 35

"Hmm, it's hot in here," Kate said, looking from Alexa to Ryan the next day as she entered the office.

"Really?" Lilith said, putting on her sweater. "I think it's rather cool."

Kate started to explain what she meant, then realized it would do no good. Lilith was clueless. Instead, Kate looked over at Frank, who gave her a knowing smile and nod.

"So, what's the plan?" Lilith asked, pulling up a chair to the work table. Kate sat in a chair next to her.

"Yes, do tell," Kate said, staring at Alexa and fluttering her eyes, faced propped in her hand, elbow resting on the table. Alexa avoided Kate's doe eyes, knowing she'd start giggling if she fell into their spell.

"Well," Alexa began, clearing her throat, "we decided for the second round of interviews, it's better if you and Nana Kate aren't there – too many people. We'll conduct the questioning in either a conference room or the interview room. Depends on what we can schedule."

"So, you and Ryan will be doing it … umm … them?" Kate asked.

"No," Alexa snapped, turning to Kate. "Uh, I mean, yes." She paused, trying to remain calm.

Frank coughed to disguise a chuckle. Ryan studied his shoes.

"Well, which is it?" Kate persisted, smiling.

"No, to your innuendo," Alexa sighed, "but yes to who will conduct the interviews."

"What innuendo?" Lilith asked, looking from Alexa to Kate, perplexed. "What are you talking about?" Alexa's eyes pleaded with Kate not to spill the beans.

"Oh nothing, dear," Kate responded. "Let's get back to business."

"I think I should be in on the interview of Eddie," Frank said firmly, arms crossed over his chest.

"Agreed," Ryan said.

"We're going to talk to the sisters first," Alexa said. "They're coming in this morning. Tony's set up for tomorrow, and Eddie will come in the next day. After each round, Ryan and I will see if we need to adjust the questions we have for Eddie. I think he's pivotal in solving this thing. Just need to get him to tell the truth. He's hiding something."

"Oh, he'll tell me the truth," Frank said. "I have a way with liars."

"I'll just bet you do," Kate said, patting his forearm. Alexa noticed Frank's blush as he turned to walk over to the coffee stand.

Colleen and Mary arrived promptly at ten o'clock. Alexa met them in the vestibule of the building and escorted them to a conference room, three pairs of heels clicking along the marble floor. She explained that Kate and Lilith would meet them after their talk to take them to lunch.

"So, how can we help?" Colleen asked, once they were seated around the table.

"We're trying to fill in some gaps about the night Julia was killed," Alexa responded. "I know we're asking a lot, trying to pull up such old memories."

"Hey, it's not the long-term memory that's such a problem," Colleen said, chuckling. "Things we did when we were kids sometimes seem like they happened last week. It's remembering what we had for lunch yesterday that gives us problems."

Mary nodded her head, smiling.

"Okay, then," Alexa said, returning the sisters' smiles. "So, I'm curious about your visit with Tony. What did he tell you guys after you left the cemetery?"

"He's such a dear man," Mary started. "Really wish he would have approached us at Mom's grave years ago. He said such lovely things about her."

"Did he say anything about that night?" Alexa persisted.

"Just that Mom had been at The Club, and sang while he played the piano," Colleen said. "He said she left earlier than usual, blowing him a kiss. Said if he'd known that was the last time he'd see her, he would have trapped her kiss in a special box." Colleen smiled, shaking her head. "I really think he had a crush on her."

"He told you guys about her singing at The Club?" Alexa asked.

"Hey, we're not that naive," Colleen said. "We pushed him a bit on where they performed together, and he told us. No big deal."

"Did he say whether she left The Club with anyone that night?" Ryan asked.

"No." The sisters looked at each other before Colleen asked, "Do you think she did? Could it have been the person who murdered her? What do you guys know? We're all adults here. We know Mom wasn't perfect. I've suspected for years she fooled around when she disappeared for days. Nothing you say can shock me. Now be honest."

Alexa glanced from the sisters to Ryan. He nodded.

"Tony was probably more candid with us than he was with you," Alexa said, after clearing her throat. "He told us your mom usually met a man at The Club and left with him. She was with him that night."

"Well, who was it?" Colleen insisted.

"Nick Jamison."

Mary's hands clutched her blouse near her heart, eyes moistening. Colleen looked down at her lap, studying folded hands. Colleen's eyes narrowed as she looked up at Alexa and Ryan. Her clenched jaw muscles twitched.

"I never trusted that son of a bitch," Colleen said flatly. "Always sniffing around Mom at those football games."

"Colleen," Mary shouted, dropping her hands to the table. "What a crude thing to say."

"Oh, stop being such a namby-pamby. You know mom wasn't a saint, for Pete's sake. It's time you stop pretending."

"She was a great Mom," Mary protested. "Sure, she had her bad moments. But for the most part, she was there for us." She paused. "Now Dad ... he could be down-right scary at times."

"Now, don't get yourself in a twitter," Colleen sighed, patting her sister's hand. "We just need to face the facts to help Alexa find the truth."

"So, your Dad had a temper?" Ryan asked, looking directly at Mary.

"Mom used to call him Mr. Bluster. He'd rant and rave about guys at work, or something he read in the paper. Didn't have any tolerance for people's faults – like lying, or cheating, or thievery, or killing. Used to say it was a good thing he wasn't a cop."

"Why's that?"

"Because he'd want to beat the crap out of them."

"How did he discipline you guys?" Ryan asked.

"Oh, if you're asking whether he beat us," Colleen interjected, "I'd have to say, no. We got our share of spankings, though."

"Now who's being a namby-pamby," Mary said, glancing at Colleen before turning back to Ryan. "He'd get out the belt every now and then. Not often, though. We'd have to do something really bad for that."

"Like what?"

"Well, I remember one time when Jack was about twelve. Mom wasn't home, but her car was in the driveway. Jack found the keys and drove it up and down the driveway. He didn't go out in the street. Just up and back. One of the neighbors saw him as he was pulling the car up to the garage, jumped to the conclusion Jack had taken it out for a drive, and told Dad. Dad was furious. Wouldn't even listen to Jack. Just got out the belt, yelling, 'Don't think you're too old for me to whip you.' He grabbed Jack, forcing him over his lap, and beat him with that damned belt ... several times. Jack never cried though." Mary looked down at her hands, folded on the table.

"Did he ever hit you ladies with the belt?" Ryan asked.

"Only once," Colleen answered. "I was a bit of a wild child. Hung out with some kids who tested the limits. I was supposed to be at some school function ... a basketball game, I think. Instead, I met up with some friends and we went joy riding. Again, one of the neighbors saw me hanging out in the parking lot of this burger joint, smoking. She told Mom and Dad.

"When I came home, Mom asked me about the game. Of course I lied. Dad whipped off his belt. Mom tried to stop him, but he just pushed her aside. Put me over his lap and gave me a couple of good whacks." She paused before continuing. "Funny thing. I don't remember him ever taking the belt to Tommy or

152

Mary." She looked over at Mary, who shook her head. Ryan looked at Alexa, imperceptibly nodding.

"Let's get back to the night of Julia's murder," Alexa said. "What do you guys remember about that night?"

"Since Mom wasn't home, I fixed supper," Colleen said. "Jack had a football game that night. A home game. He left before us, driving Mom's car. The rest of us piled into Dad's, and we went to the game. Don't remember who won. We went to bed soon after we got home. I don't remember anything else happening, until the next morning."

"Well, I do," Mary said.

Colleen looked over at her sister, surprised.

"How do you remember back that far?" Colleen asked.

"When Dad died, I had some anxiety issues. I ended up going to a counselor. She helped me deal with some repressed memories. Mostly they had to do with Mom's death."

"Really? You never told me that."

"Hey, we may be sisters, but you don't have to know everything that's going on in my head."

Colleen stared at her sister, tight-lipped. Mary returned the stare.

"So, what do you remember?" Alexa prompted, interrupting the stare-off.

"I woke up sometime in the middle of the night," Mary said, turning to Alexa and Ryan. "I heard Dad yelling downstairs. I got out of bed and listened at the bedroom door. I didn't dare go down."

"You never told me about that, either," Colleen said.

"Never thought it was important. I mean, why bring up bad memories?"

"Who was he yelling at?" Ryan asked.

"I don't know. It might have been someone from his work."

"Did you hear a male or female voice?"

"Oh, it was definitely a man." Mary paused, finger tapping her lips. "Wait a minute; I did hear Dad yell a name. It was Greg. Must have been that awful Greg Lyons."

"Do you remember anything they said?" Alexa asked.

"Hmm. Let's see. Mostly what I remember were the shouted words. Dad called Greg a god-damned liar. Then Greg shouted that he knew what he saw."

"Did he say what he saw?" Ryan asked.

Mary closed her eyes, tilting her head back and forth. Seconds ticked by as she searched her memory.

"I remember Mom's name being said," Mary answered as she opened her eyes. "Yeah. He yelled that he saw her leaving some place with …" Mary concentrated on her hands. "With Nick. Oh my god," she said, face buried in her hands. Wiping away a tear, she cleared her throat before continuing.

"Dad yelled at him that it was none of his damned business. Called him a few choice names. Then I heard the front door slam. I heard Dad's steps coming up, so I scampered back into bed. He opened the door like he was checking on us, then closed it. He went to the boys' room, too. And then I heard him go back downstairs."

"Did you hear him leave the house?" Ryan asked.

"No. I lay there, not getting back to sleep for some time. I finally heard him come back up the stairs and go to his room. I fell asleep soon after that."

"Is it possible he left after you went back to sleep?"

"Not likely," Mary said, shaking her head. "I'm a pretty light sleeper. Always was."

"Hold on a sec," Colleen said. "You guys aren't thinking Dad had anything to do with Mom's death, are you?"

"We're just trying to get the full picture of what happened," Alexa responded.

"Well, you're way off track," Colleen said, voice shaking with anger. "Dad adored Mom. He may have hit us kids from time to time … usually when we deserved it. But he never laid a hand on Mom in anger. He put up with her disappearances for years. As I told you before, even in his last years, he always defended her. There is just no way he could have done anything to her." Colleen tapped her index finger on the table.

"You know," she continued, "maybe you should look at Greg Lyons."

"Why's that?" Alexa asked.

"I remember the week before; he was at Jack's football game. He sat down next to Dad, obviously drunk. Slurring and talking loud. Mom said something to Dad. Then Dad told Greg to leave." She paused, thinking. "Greg stumbled over to where Nick and Rosie were sitting. Started hanging all over

Rosie. Nick didn't seem to mind. I remember being glad he was away from us. He stank." Colleen crinkled her nose at the memory.

"Okay then," Alexa said, jotting a note. "Now, what do you remember about the morning after your Dad had the fight with Greg … the night …?" Her voice trailed off.

"We got up, as usual," Colleen said, sighing. "Since it was a Saturday, we all had plans. Jack was going to football practice. Asked if he could take Mom's car. Dad said no … that he could ride his bike. I went to hang out with some of my friends at the park. Tommy had a piano lesson. Don't remember what you did, Mary."

"One of my friends came over to play," Mary responded. "Dad stayed home to watch us." She paused. "In fact, I was there when the police car came to our house. I was up in my bedroom, playing, and saw it pull up from my window. Dad answered the door after the officers rang the bell. The next thing I heard was Dad yelling, 'No.' It wasn't his usual, angry tone. More mournful. I ran from my room, leaving my friend behind, and raced down the stairs. Dad's head was in his hands. The officers were just staring at him. When he noticed I was there, he looked at me. He was crying. I'll never forget the look on his face." Mary gulped to hold back her own tears.

"After the officers left, Dad took me into the living room, and sat next to me on the couch. All he told me was something had happened to Mom, and he needed to go downtown. He told me to go over to my friend's house to continue playing. Wouldn't tell me what happened. Just that he'd be back for supper, and I shouldn't worry. I asked if Mom would be home for supper, but he didn't answer. Just shuffled me off to go with my friend."

"So, when did he tell you what happened?" Alexa asked.

"After supper," Colleen answered. "I remember he didn't eat, and I asked whether I had cooked something wrong. He quietly told me everything was fine. He was so quiet. Jack, of course, wasn't home for supper. Dad asked us all to go into the living room when we were done eating. That's when he told us Mom was dead. Said it was an accident. He also told us Jack was in the hospital. We all cried and hugged each other."

"How did you learn it really wasn't an accident?" Alexa asked.

"After Tommy and Mary left the room, I pushed Dad on the details. I remember thinking I was so grown up, since I was fifteen." Colleen chuckled. "He finally told me she was killed, and about Jack seeing her. He started sobbing, so I left and went up to my room. Mary and Tommy were in there, still crying. The rest is a bit of a blur. I do remember people … family and friends … coming and going the next week or so. It was just such a sad time." Colleen reached over and held Mary's hand, then looked straight at Alexa and Ryan.

"You know you should be looking into Nick's role in all this, too," Colleen said. "I do remember Dad yelling at him and Rosie when they came to the house after the funeral. Couldn't hear what he said. I was heading to the kitchen."

"I remember," Mary whispered. "Dad followed them outside and punched Nick in the face."

"What?" Colleen and Alexa said together, heads whipping to face Mary.

"I was near the living room window and looked out. Dad was screaming at them. He walked right up to Nick and punched him. Several men grabbed Dad and pushed Nick away. Dad was straining against their hold. I could hear him yelling to let him go."

"What did Nick do?" Alexa asked.

"Nothing. He didn't try to hit back. Rosie screamed, of course. But Nick just stood there with his hand to his jaw. Then he grabbed Rosie and headed to their car."

"Did you hear what your Dad said to Nick?" Ryan asked.

"Just bits and pieces … only when he was yelling really loud. He said something like how dare they show up to his house. And something about everything being all Nick's fault. Then he punched him. After Nick and Rosie left, a couple of the men stood outside talking to Dad before they came back in the house. I ran over to him and he just held me." Mary lowered her head.

"I'm so sorry we had to stir up these memories," Alexa said. "There's only one other question we have for you."

"What's that?" Colleen asked.

"When Mom and I did some research in to the newspapers from back then, there was mention of your Dad's possible ties to the Irish mob. Do you think they could have been involved in Julia's death?"

A strained chuckle escaped as Colleen sat back in her chair.

"I remember seeing those articles," she said. "Just a bunch of poppy-cock. Dad subcontracted on some Charles River development projects back then. Sure, there was lots of graft going around. It was a big project. But it all went to either the primary contractors or the politicians." Colleen sighed and shook her head. "That Sean O'Connor, the Irish mob up-and-comer from back then, was a mean son-of-a-bitch. But he wouldn't have even known who Dad was. Dad's business was small potatoes. And Mary's right. Dad was a 'Mr. Bluster'. I remember him ranting about how crooked some people were. But he'd never do anything about it. Never piss anyone off enough to lose his contract. It paid the bills, and he had his family. We always came first with him."

"Well, I think that's all we have," Alexa said, glancing at Ryan for assurance. He nodded before she looked back at the sisters. "Again, I'm sorry we had to dredge up some painful memories."

"It's okay," Colleen said. "I just hope it helps you find out what happened. Please keep us in the loop."

Alexa escorted Colleen and Mary to the vestibule. Kate and Lilith were there to meet them for their lunch date – with a surprise. Lilith introduced the sisters to Johnny. They gasped at his resemblance to Jack, as the dam to their emotions finally cracked. Weeping, they hugged him tightly.

CHAPTER 36

"**M**y money's on Nick," Ryan said when they returned to the office.

"I don't know," Alexa responded. "I'm not convinced he was capable of murdering her. I mean, it sounded like he didn't even defend himself against Dan's assault. Plus, if he killed her, would he show up at her funeral and house afterwards?"

"Maybe he was trying to look like the good guy to avert attention," Ryan countered. "Let's look at what we have so far. Nick had ample opportunity."

"But no motive."

"Maybe Julia was ending the affair. If he was so crazy about her, it might make him snap."

"From what Tony told us before," Alexa said, "that's unlikely. Even if she did end it, would Nick be that upset? He probably knew she wasn't ever going to leave Dan. They'd been carrying on for years." Alexa paused, eyes rolling to the ceiling. "You know, we shouldn't eliminate Tony. Sure, he's a nice old guy now. But he obviously carried a torch for Julia. Maybe seeing her with Nick that night was a last straw for him. Maybe he went over to Nick's apartment after work, saw them together, and went crazy jealous."

"Or maybe he got there earlier, and that was the skirmish the neighbors complained about," Ryan added. "We need to push him a bit during the interview tomorrow."

"And there's Greg Lyons," Alexa said. "According to the interview notes, he said he saw Julia with Nick. Maybe he followed them out of The Club, and attacked them."

"Hmm," Ryan said, stroking his chin in the manner of all great thinkers.

As he wandered over to the coffee stand, Ryan turned his head around toward Alexa, reverting to cop-talk. "Djeat?"

"No, djou?" Alexa fell into the familiar prattle, chuckling.

"Djwanna go someplace?"

"Umm, can't. Mom's expecting me for dinner. Take another rain check though." She smiled broadly at him.

The following afternoon, Tony arrived promptly for his eleven o'clock appointment. Ryan escorted him to the conference room.

"Thanks for coming in," Alexa said. "We just want to plug some holes in the investigation."

"Hey, anything to get to the bottom of who killed Julia," Tony responded. He sat back in the chair, legs crossed, arms folded over his knee.

"Okay, then," Ryan said. "You said on the night of her murder, Julia left The Club with Nick at around nine o'clock. Right?"

"Yes."

"How'd you know what time it was?"

"I'd just come off break. Did forty-minute sets, starting at eight, ending at midnight. I'd break for about fifteen minutes between sets. Julia and Nick left just after I'd started my second set."

"Did Julia usually blow you a kiss when she left?" Ryan asked.

"Nope. She usually stayed until I was finished for the evening. Liked singing with me. She'd give me a cheek kiss before leaving."

"You said sometimes she'd go home with you," Alexa said. "Why not that night?"

"She was still in her upbeat mood," Tony responded. "She'd only stay with me when she was blue. Then she'd go home the next day."

"Do you know where Nick took her?" Ryan asked.

"I guess to his apartment."

"Did you know where? Did Julia ever tell you?"

"She did say he had some ritzy place," Tony said, pausing to stroke his chin. "Think it might have been on Marlborough Street. Right around the corner from The Club."

"Did you see anyone follow them when they left?" Ryan asked.

"Not that I remember. But there were so many people coming in and out." He stopped, tapping his nose in thought.

"There was one fellow who seemed interested in her. Asked me about who she was during my break. Thought maybe it was one of her fans. When I told him her name, he just smiled and said something about wondering whether Dan knew."

Ryan and Alexa exchanged glances.

"Did this guy follow them out?" Ryan asked.

"Don't think so. Think he was still at the bar after they left."

"But you're not sure?"

"Let me think about it a bit." Tony looked up at the ceiling as if it held answers, alternately stoking his chin and tapping his lips with his fore finger. After a minute, he snapped his fingers and looked back at Ryan.

"I know he stuck around. I remember he got kicked out about an hour later." Tony chuckled at the memory. "He was a real loud-mouth. Said something inappropriate to one of the bar maids. As the bouncer was pulling him off his chair, he yelled something like, 'Sure, it's fine for a man's wife to carry on an affair here. You'll be sorry when I tell her husband.' Then he shrugged off the bouncer, straightened his lapels, and stumbled out of the place. Geez, I had forgotten about that until now. Think it means anything?"

"Dunno," Ryan said, shrugging. "Do you remember the guy's name? Did he frequent The Club?"

"Boy, you're really tapping into my long-term memory here," Tony chuckled. He closed his eyes for a few seconds, thinking. Opening his eyes, he pursed his lips. "Greg something? An animal last name. Joke around The Club was he'd purr at the ladies and roar at the men."

"Could it have been Lyons?" Alexa asked.

"Yeah, that sounds about right. He wasn't a regular, but did come in about once a week, or so. Hung out with some of the younger crowd – guys barely old enough to drink."

"Think any of his buddies are still around?"

"Drunks will always find someplace to hang out. They form a warped sense of fraternity. Those who are still alive are probably hanging around some seedy bar in the same neighborhood."

Movement from Alexa's leg caught Ryan's attention. It appeared to be keeping time with some thought pattern she was developing. He'd ask her about it after the interview.

Looking down at his notes, then back at Tony, Ryan leaned forward as he asked, "Did Nick's wife ever come into The Club?"

"You must be kidding," Tony answered with a slight twitter. "The Club was Nick's place. He'd never bring her in there." He paused before continuing. "Julia did tell me about her though. Said she was a real, um, bitch. Told me about their history. How she dated Nick before meeting Dan, and how Rosie moved in on Nick afterwards."

"Do you know whether Rosie knew about Nick's infidelities?" Alexa asked.

"I'm not certain. I did ask Julia about what she thought Rosie would do if she found out about Nick. She just laughed and said Rosie knew about his fooling around. As long as Rosie got to spend his money, she didn't really care. Plus, Julia was certain about Nick being able to keep secrets. Like keeping the apartment a secret from Rosie. And, Rosie was no saint. Julia told me she'd seen Rosie with other men." Tony shook his head. "Strange bed-fellows, I guess."

"You loved Julia, didn't you?" Alexa asked, starting an alternate line of questioning.

"Yeah."

"Were you jealous of her relationship with Nick?"

"Naw," Tony replied. "Now don't get me wrong. I didn't really approve of her relationship with Nick. Thought she was cheapening herself." He chuckled before continuing. "But then, who am I to judge what others do?"

"Are you sure Julia and Nick went to his apartment that night?" Ryan asked, switching topics again.

"Only said I saw them leave. Just assuming they went to his place."

"Why would you assume that? Isn't it possible they went somewhere else?"

"Julia told me that's where they always went. She'd try to tell me details ... like I was some girlfriend. But I'd wave her off." Tony chuckled again. "Kind of a game we used to play."

"So, you didn't follow them there?" Ryan asked.

"What? No." Tony paused, looking from Ryan to Alexa. A smile crinkled his face. "Are you guys thinking I had something to do with Julia's murder? That maybe I followed them and killed her in a jealous rage?" He paused again. "Now, I admit I loved Julia. But not as a lover. She wasn't my type."

Tony leaned back in his chair, arms placed across his stomach as it jumped up and down with laughter. He bent forward, wiping tears from his eyes. Alexa and Ryan stared at him, not knowing the cause of his mirth.

"For Pete's sake," Tony said, catching his breath. "Don't you guys know? What kind of detectives are you? I'm gay as the day is long."

CHAPTER **37**

"**D**o you believe those two shmoes didn't know I was gay?" Tony asked Lilith as they walked out of the police station.

"You are?" Lilith asked, giggling to hide her embarrassment.

"Oh my, what a bunch you are," Tony chuckled. "Rather clueless aren't you? Well anyway, let's go have that duck boat ride." Lilith hooked her arm into his as they strolled to the parking lot.

"Well, that was a bit of a dead end," Alexa said when they returned to the office. "Except for the reference to Greg seeing Julia and Nick at The Club. Curious that he was kicked out about an hour later. I wonder if he went directly to Dan's house."

"Yeah," Ryan said, "Or if the fight was enough to provoke Dan into going downtown."

"But Mary said she would have heard if he left the house. Plus, chances are slim that Dan would have known where Nick's apartment was." Alexa shook her head. "No, I'm thinking more and more that Dan should be ruled out as a suspect." She paused before continuing, "And hey, what about Tony's revelation? I didn't have a clue he wasn't straight."

"I did," Ryan said.

"Oh, you did not."

"Well, I suspected it. Just didn't want to make a big deal of it."

"You are such a fibber," Alexa said, grinning. "You're the one who thought he might have killed Julia in a jealous rage."

"Yeah, but maybe because he had a thing for Nick," Ryan said, cocking his head.

"I give up," Alexa said, raising her arms.

"Hey, what was with the questions about Greg Lyons?" Ryan asked. "You developing some theory you want to share?"

165

"Just an intuition – nothing solid. I'll run it by you after we talk with Eddie." Alexa paged through her notes. "Let's see what more we have here before tomorrow's interview." Head down, she didn't notice Frank's entrance.

"So, you guys ready to go over what we're gonna ask Eddie?" Frank asked. For the next two hours, Ryan and Alexa briefed Frank on their interviews with the sisters and Tony.

"We really need to push him on several points here," Frank said. "Remember, he useta be a cop ... granted, not a very good one. He learned a thing or two about interviewing techniques. I'll handle things when we really need to cut through his bull-shit." Alexa and Ryan agreed.

Eddie flipped open a black wallet-sized leather container, displaying his tarnished shield to the security officer. He didn't have many opportunities to show off his retired officer's badge. When Frank arrived in the building's vestibule, Eddie was telling stories of his make-believe bravery to several young officers. Rolling his eyes at the officers, Frank escorted Eddie to the interview room. The conference room used to interview the sisters and Tony was not available. The sparse furnishings and smaller floor space of the interview room better suited their line of questioning with Eddie.

"What's with the interrogation technique, using this hole of a room?" Eddie asked. "Thought we was just gonna have a friendly chat." He pulled his cigarette pack from his shirt pocket.

"No smoking," Frank said, flatly.

"Aw, come on," Eddie whined.

"Sorry. Rules against smoking in government buildings."

Eddie sighed as he shoved his pack into his pocket.

"We just need to clear up a few things you told us," Alexa explained. "We're trying to put all the puzzle pieces together in Julia's murder."

"Don't know what else I can help you with," Eddie said, smirking. "Investigated it as much as we could years ago. Hate to tell you, but it's a dead end case." He sat back in his chair, tipping it on its rear legs, the back leaning against the wall.

"Careful," Frank said, returning Eddie's smirk. "You might tip over and hurt yourself." Eddie shifted his weight forward, bringing the chair back down on its front legs.

"Let's start with the night of the domestic disturbance in Nick's apartment," Alexa said, shifting through her notes.

"Yeah, what about it?" Eddie asked, eyes narrowing.

"You said when you responded to the call, you didn't know it was Nick's apartment until you got there. Right?"

"Yeah."

"Yet you knew Nick had girlfriends. Where did you think he took them?"

"Didn't know. Figured he had a place. Or maybe he sprung for hotel rooms." Eddie pulled out his cigarettes, rotating taps along the pack's edges on the table.

"Come on now, Eddie," Frank interjected. "Nick made good money, but not enough to afford hotel rooms every time he met a lady. He was a smart guy. Wouldn't spend more than he had to for nights of enjoyment." Frank's eyebrows furled as he leaned into Eddie.

"Okay," Eddie chuckled. "Maybe I did know he had a place. But I didn't know where. He didn't want Rosie finding out, so he wouldn't tell no one. Not even me. Asked him one time if I could use it. Said no. Just like that. Wouldn't even consider it."

Frank sat back in his chair, and nodded to Alexa and Ryan to continue the questions. A toothpick slowly rotated in his mouth.

"So you were completely surprised when he opened the door?" Alexa asked.

"Yeah."

"And you said he was alone?"

"Yeah." The cigarette pack double-tapped on the table.

"Didn't hear any voices? Maybe someone who would be curious about the cops being at the door?"

"Nope." Another double tap.

"You also said Nick was holding a towel with ice to his head. That he'd hit his head when he slipped coming out of the shower. Right?" Alexa asked, cocking her left eyebrow.

"Yeah." Tap, tap.

"Let's shift things a bit here," Ryan said. "Do you know where Nick met ladies?"

"Oh, lots a places," Eddie said, placing the cigarette pack on the table. "Mostly bars, I guess."

"Any one in particular?"

"He liked upscale joints. Classy guy that Nick. Wouldn't go to no honky-tonks." Eddie paused, rolling his eyes to the ceiling. Looking back at Ryan, he continued. "Remember he liked a place called The Club. Liked the name of it, too. Said he could tell Rosie he was going to the club and she'd think he was headed to the country club." Eddie chuckled. "She was a real flutter-brain."

Frank smirked.

"Did you ever go to The Club?" Ryan asked.

"Maybe a couple a times. A bit too classy for my taste."

"Ever go there with Nick?"

"Naw. By the time I was old enough to go out to clubs, Nick was done going to The Club."

"When did he stop going there?" Alexa asked.

"Dunno," Eddie responded, shrugging his shoulders. "Don't really matter. He just started going to other places."

"Let's skip to the day Julia's body was found," Ryan said, looking down at his notes. "You met Nick that day for lunch." Ryan looked straight into Eddie's eyes. "In your discussions with him that afternoon, did he tell you he had been at The Club the night before?"

"He mighta mentioned it." Eddie licked his lips. "Mostly we talked about his secret apartment, and the dolls he took there."

"Did he mention he was with Julia the night before, at The Club?"

"No." He picked up the cigarette pack again, tapping it twice on its side.

"Okay then," Ryan said, then glanced back at his notes. "You heard the call on the radio and responded. Since your partner was the first senior officer on site, the two of you caught the case."

"That's right," Eddie said. "As I told you before, we interviewed everyone we could think of. All dead ends. Autopsy just showed she'd been strangled. No prints. No nothing."

"So, you never saw the rest of her clothes?"

"Nope." Tap, tap.

"Let's back up a bit," Alexa said. Eddie leered at her. "You said you interviewed Greg Lyons during the investigation. He told you he saw Julia leave The Club that night." She leaned toward him. "Are you sure Nick didn't tell you he was with her? That he left with her?"

"Look, I told you Nick never told me he was with Julia." Tap, tap. "And Greg never said who he'd seen her with." Tap, tap. Eddie turned to Ryan, face flushed.

"Were you on the detail at Julia's funeral?" Ryan asked.

"Sure was," Eddie said, face returning to its normal, grey hue. "Wanted to see if anyone did anything suspicious. Didn't notice nothing."

"I understand Nick and Rosie were there, and they went to the O'Shea's house after the cemetery services."

"Yeah, they was there." Eddie started fidgeting with the cigarette pack, rolling it from side to side.

"If they weren't friends with Dan and Julia," Ryan persisted, "why do you think they were there?"

"Dunno. Just outta respect, I guess." Tap, tap.

"Were you at the house when Dan punched Nick?" Alexa asked. Eddie narrowed his eyes as he turned to her.

"Yeah. Dunno what come over Dan. He just started yelling at 'em, telling 'em to get outta his house. Then he followed 'em out, and cold-cocked Nick. Some of the guys grabbed Dan, and I pushed Nick away. Told him they should leave. Rosie was screaming her head off. Nick just took her by the arm, got in the car, and drove off."

"Now, why do you think Dan would hit Nick?"

"Not sure," Eddie said, shaking his head. "There was bad blood between them … from the past, you know." Tap, tap.

"I read in an old newspaper that Dan might have had connections to the Irish mob," Alexa said, leaning forward. "Your report from back then doesn't mention anything about that. Any idea where the papers would get such information?"

"Well, construction back then was loaded with roughnecks. Hadta been big and bullish to do that kinda work. Dan hired 'em. Probably knew a bunch of 'em from his high school days. Don't know how many were connected, though. Sean O'Connor was known for hiring some of the biggest and baddest for his gang. Trying to make a name for hisself. Went around threatening and beating up folks back then. But they pretty much stayed away from the construction roughnecks. Kinda respect thing going with 'em." Eddie paused to snicker.

"Unless, of course, they owed money or did something stupid like pounding on someone's sister. Lotsa people back then thought that if someone was big and tough, they hadta be connected. Not so." Eddie shook his head for emphasis. "Lotsa people thought everyone associated with the Charles River project was crooked. And, lotsa people got put outta their homes on that project. But it was a slum. To be honest, I don't think Dan woulda got caught up in any of that stuff. He really was a decent guy." Eddie lowered his head, coughed, then looked up.

"Say," Eddie continued, "can I getta soda? My throat's getting awful dry with all this talking." He chuckled nervously.

"Sure thing," Frank said, standing up.

"Think I'll go for a smoke," Eddie said, starting to rise up from his chair.

"Don't think so," Frank said, motioning for Eddie to remain seated. "We won't be much longer." Frank opened the door, looking down the corridor. "Hey Sully, get us a couple a sodas, will ya?"

Alexa and Ryan pushed their chairs back, the metal legs emitting a screech along the floor. They stretched, then repositioned themselves to sit on either side of Frank. It was his turn to take the lead.

CHAPTER **38**

F rank wandered around the room, stretching his back. He answered the knock at the door, bringing the sodas to the table. Handing one to Eddie, he popped open the other can and took a slug.

"I just want to clarify a couple of things," Frank said, sitting directly across from Eddie. "Let's start with the day of the funeral. Why, exactly, do you think Nick and Rosie went to the funeral and the O'Shea's house?"

"Like I said," Eddie responded, "outta respect." He picked up the cigarette pack, tapping it twice on one side.

"Come on, Eddie. You said there was bad blood between the Jamison's and O'Shea's. Weren't you just a bit surprised to see them there?"

"Yeah, guess I was."

"So, you didn't ask Nick why they were there, or say something to him after Dan hit him?" Frank asked.

"Hmm. Guess I mighta." Eddie blinked rapidly, and then his eyes shifted down to stare at the cigarette pack. "When I suggested Nick take Rosie home, I think I asked him why they'd come there. Rosie overheard, and hissed at me and Nick. Said something about it being all his idea. Said she'd as soon spit on Julia's grave. Remember Nick's face got all red. Looked like he was gonna slap her. He grabbed her arm, real forceful like, told her to shut up and get in the car. She said something back to him about how she wasn't scared of him ... knew she could take him on. Then he asked me whether we'd seen anyone suspicious. Knew us cops were there to look around. Also asked if I'd keep him in the loop."

"So, did you?" Frank asked.

"Talked to him about the case a couple of times over lunch ... and once at his house. Told him how frustrated I was with the case. About getting nowhere with the interviews."

"Did he offer you any advice?"

"That night at his house, couple a weeks later, he mighta suggested the case be dropped."

"And was it?" Frank asked.

"Coupla months later. Nick was right. Even took me out for a drink to commiserate. Said some things are better left not solved." Eddie shook his head. "Remember Dan being really pissed when Billy and me went over to his house to let him know we was dropping the case. Can't really blame him."

"What did you hear at the O'Shea's house before Dan hit Nick?" Frank asked. "What provoked Dan?"

"Nothing." Tap, tap.

"Did Nick ever mention he'd been with Julia the night before she was found dead?" Frank asked.

"Nope." Tap, tap.

Frank looked down at his hands, shaking his head. Taking the toothpick out of his mouth, he looked straight at Eddie.

"Eddie, Eddie, Eddie," Frank started. "You know I can tell when you're lying, don't ya?"

"Whaddya mean?" Eddie asked, beads of sweat forming on his upper lip.

"You have a 'tell'."

"Huh?"

"Every time you lie, you tap your cigarette pack on the table ... twice." Frank grinned at Eddie. "So, let's try this again. What provoked Dan into hitting Nick?"

"Hell if I know." Eddie sat back in his chair, folding his arms across his chest.

Frank extended his arms across the table, leaning forward.

"Don't give me that crap," Frank said, voice strained. "You were a cop. You know the score here. I'll prove you had a part in covering up this murder. Get you charged as an accessory after the fact. Maybe even throw in an obstructing justice charge. Convicted on those charges alone might threaten your pension. How do you think your ex would react if she stopped getting paid?"

Eddie leaned forward, dropping his arms to his lap. Moisture appeared on his forehead and upper lip.

"Okay, okay, man," he said. "I'll tell ya what I know. But it ain't much." Eddie coughed before continuing.

"I was standing outside when I heard Dan yelling. Next thing I know, Nick and Rosie was coming outta the house, real fast. Dan was right behind them. I heard him call Nick a low-life son-of-a-bitch. Said it was his fault Julia was dead. Said he just couldn't leave her alone, could he. Took advantage of her. Knew she was fragile, but still couldn't keep his hands offa her. Then Dan punched him. Took several guys to pull Dan back. He was a bull of a guy back then."

"What was Rosie's reaction to what Dan was saying?"

"Nothing much. She just kinda stood there looking from Dan to Nick. Had that stupid stare thing going. You know, wide eyes, mouth open with no sound coming out. Except for that shriek when Dan hit Nick." Eddie took a slug from his soda can. "I went over to Nick and Rosie when the guys had Dan restrained. Rosie kept saying over and over that Nick had nothing to do with it. She'd vouch for him. Said he was with her."

"So, when did Nick tell you he had been with Julia?" Frank asked.

"Not that day. Woulda sent Rosie into another frenzy. But he'd already told me about him and Julia. Told me he saw her several times a year at The Club."

"Did he tell you he took her back to his apartment?"

"Said they'd been intimate. Just assumed he'd taken her there when they met up. But he didn't say nothing about taking her there that night. Honest to Pete."

"But someone else did, right?" Frank asked, leaning closer to Eddie.

"Whaddya mean?" Eddie asked, forehead glistening with sweat.

"Greg Lyons told you he saw Julia leaving with Nick, didn't he? And that he told Dan later that night." Frank paused, eyelids squinting. "It's in your report, Eddie. So don't lie."

"Okay, okay. Yeah. Greg told us he'd seen Julia leave with Nick."

"What time did he say he told Dan?"

"I dunno. Guess around ten or eleven. Honest to Pete, I can't remember." Eddie coughed into his hand.

"Was Julia there when you went to the apartment?" Frank asked.

"Dunno."

"Eddie," Frank said, dragging out the name.

"Honest to Pete. Didn't see or hear her."

"You went into the apartment?"

"Nope. Just stood at the door talking to Nick."

"Was there someone else there?" Frank asked.

"Not sure," Eddie replied, eyes blinking. He reached for his cigarette pack, then jerked his hand back as if the pack was on fire.

"I'll ask again," Frank sighed. "Was there someone else at the apartment with Nick?"

"Okay, yeah. I heard a woman's voice asking Nick who was at the door."

"Did you recognize the voice?"

"Yeah." Eddie sucked in his lips, forming a thin line across his face.

"Come on, Eddie. Don't make me pull it out of you."

"Okay, okay. It was Rosie. Couldn't never mistake her whiny voice for no one else."

"Did you see her?"

"She came to the door."

"What did you think when you saw her?" Frank asked, leaning into Eddie.

"Must admit, I was surprised. I mean, that was Nick's place – where he'd take his girlies. Didn't know Rosie knew about it."

"So, what happened when you saw her?"

"She said hi. Then held up something in her hand and asked Nick what she should do with them. He laughed and told her to put them on."

"What was she holding?" Frank asked.

"Looked like women's lingerie. You know ... hose and panties ... maybe a nightie or slip."

Ryan leaned back in his chair, looking over at Alexa. She returned his glance, eyebrows raised.

CHAPTER 39

"Can I go now?" Eddie whined. "I really need a smoke."

"Just a couple of more questions," Alexa said. Eddie glared at her.

"How well did you know Greg Lyons?" she asked.

"Knew him from the neighborhood." Eddie shrugged. "Went to school with one of his kids."

"What was he like?"

"He was okay enough. Kinda loud mouth. Useta see him in some bars. Got kicked outta plenty of them." Eddie chuckled. "Hung out with guys more his kid's age. Probably made him feel important, or something. When I was in high school, we'd go to his house to get liquored up. Thought it was cool at the time."

"Do you know where he hung out?"

"Mainly neighborhood bars. Heard that gang went into the city sometimes when they wanted to go upscale."

"Do you think any of his old buddies are still around?" Alexa asked.

"Guess so," Eddie said, then leaned toward Alexa. "You looking for a date, or something? Want me to see if I can fix you up? They'd be a bit old for you. But maybe you're into geezers."

Alexa felt the color rise in her cheeks.

"That's enough," Frank said before she had a chance to respond.

"Just teasing her a bit," Eddie said, open hands facing upward. "Gotta learn to take it if you're gonna be around cops and bad guys." He barred his yellowed teeth as he grinned.

"Got any more questions for Eddie?" Frank asked, looking at Ryan and Alexa. Both shrugged their shoulders, shaking their heads.

"Okay," Frank said. "Thanks for coming clean with us. If you think of anything else, call me."

"Sure."

Frank escorted Eddie out of the building while Ryan and Alexa returned to the office.

"Man," Alexa said, "this thing keeps getting more complicated."

"We just need to sift through all the pieces," Ryan said. "It'll come together." Grabbing cups of coffee, they sat at the work table.

"Well, I think we can rule out the mob connection," Alexa said.

"Agreed."

"And, we've pretty much ruled out Dan."

"Unless Julia did return home that night," Ryan said. "Even though Mary said she's a light sleeper, and never heard anything else, there's still a possibility that Dan killed her outside the house."

"How do you figure that?"

"Maybe he waited outside for her. Suppose she came home and he confronted her on the front lawn, or took her out back, so they wouldn't disturb the kids. He must have been pretty heated after Greg told him he'd seen her with Nick."

"Boy, I hate to admit it," Alexa said, "but that is a possibility. There's just a big part of me that feels sorry for Dan. I don't like thinking he could have done this."

"Don't let your personal feelings get mixed up with your analysis," Ryan warned. "We like to rationalize that people with low morals are always the bad guys. But bad thoughts don't always equate to bad deeds."

"Yeah, yeah, I know." Alexa sighed. "And we still don't know for sure Julia even went to Nick's apartment that night."

"But we do know – at least according to Eddie – that Rosie was there."

Alexa fingered a strand of hair, lips pursed in thought.

"You ready to tell me what you're thinking about Greg Lyon's involvement in all this?" Ryan asked.

"Sure," she said, looking at Ryan. "Something about Greg bothers me. So, here's what I'm thinking. Maybe when he was kicked out of The Club, Greg ran into Julia on the street."

"How would that happen? I'm not following you."

"If we can believe Eddie – and I'm still not sure I do – only Nick and Rosie were in the apartment when he arrived at ten. What if Nick had taken Julia there, and right when they're about to get it on, there's a knock at the door. It's Rosie. They scramble to get Julia out of the apartment before Nick opens the door. So now Julia's out on the street by herself, maybe heading back to The Club. She runs into Greg. He accosts her. She resists him. He kills her and dumps her in the Charles. Then, to cover his tracks, he goes to Dan." Alexa paused. "Plus it would explain her missing undergarments. She didn't have time to put them back on before leaving the apartment."

"Wow, you have a vivid imagination," Ryan chuckled.

"I'm serious," Alexa scowled. "You have to admit it's a possibility."

"So, how does Julia leave without being seen by Rosie?"

"Fire escape. Or maybe they hide her in the apartment – a closet – then Nick distracts Rosie while Julia slips out the front door."

"But there's no way of checking any of this out. Pure speculation."

Alexa returned to twirling her hair. She stood and paced around the room. Ryan silently watched. A couple of minutes passed before she sat next to him, eyes sparkling.

"You know, we talked about interviewing Rosie," Alexa said. "Maybe she saw Greg outside Nick's apartment building when she got there. According to Colleen, they knew each other. Maybe Rosie can actually help us turn speculation into probability."

"Okay, then. We'll see what a ninety-some woman can remember," Ryan conceded. "Too bad Greg's dead."

"Yeah, but some of his drinking buddies may still be around."

"May be," Ryan admitted. "We can check out some of the bars. One thing about drunks – they do like to brag. Maybe he told someone something useful."

Alexa's grin crinkled her eyes. Ryan scooted his chair closer.

"You know, there's another possibility we haven't even explored," Ryan said. "Perhaps the whole strangling thing was an accident."

"Huh?"

"I don't want to insult your feminine sensibilities."

"What are you talking about?" Alexa asked, facing Ryan.

"Have you ever heard of erotic asphyxiation?"

"Umm, I don't think so."

"Well, some people practice it during sexual intercourse. The premise is that cutting off oxygen to the brain increases sexual arousal."

"You have to be kidding," Alexa said, shaking her head.

"Now, stay with me here," Ryan said. "Suppose Nick and Julia were into kinky sex. Maybe he was using the scarf to choke her as a form of arousal, and it got out of hand."

"So you're saying he accidentally killed her?" Alexa's eyes widened as her eyebrows arched.

"It's a possibility."

"But that still doesn't explain why Rosie was there," Alexa said, shaking her head. "It's just not adding up in my gut." Alexa stood, pacing the room.

"Look, I need to get out of here for a bit," Alexa said, heading to the door. "Need to clear my head."

"Want some company?"

"Sure. How about we take a walk by the Charles?"

"Why there?" Ryan asked.

"The Common and Public Garden are too crowded with tourists this time of year. It's better to commune with nature where it's quieter."

"So, we're gonna commune, huh?" Ryan's eyebrows danced, eyes twinkling.

"Guess I'll have to teach you what that means," Alexa sighed, suppressing the giggle she felt churning in her stomach.

CHAPTER 40

Rather than drive, Alexa and Ryan decided to take the Massachusetts Bay Transit Authority subway – known as the "T" – from the Ruggles station to Downtown Crossing. Emerging from the station, they walked over to Park Street.

"You know one thing I love about Boston?" Alexa asked as they turned onto Beacon Street.

"What's that?"

"Its walkability. If you have the right shoes on, you can walk anywhere in the city." Both Alexa and Ryan had changed into sneakers before leaving the office.

"Yeah," Ryan said, "but its drivability stinks. The story goes that the streets are nothing more than paved cow paths. There's no rhyme or reason to how they meander around the city. Very frustrating for drivers not familiar with the streets." Passing the Boston Common, crowded with summer tourists, they walked past the Public Garden.

"I worked on the swan boats one summer," Ryan said.

"You don't say."

"Aye matey. I was the captain of a fine vessel. Arrgh."

Alexa giggled at Ryan's poor imitation of a pirate.

"The lines are probably long right now," Alexa said, glancing in the direction of the Public Garden. "But those silly platforms with park benches attached and a big swan shell on the back are an attraction that draws the tourists."

"Well, pedaling them sure kept me in shape," Ryan said.

Crossing the bridge over Storrow Drive, they headed to the Esplanade. The heat of the summer had taken a break, leaving a mild day with hints of the upcoming fall. When they arrived on the walking path along the river, heading north, Alexa slowed her stride. Strolling, she glanced up at the trees slightly spotted with color amid deep green leaves. She deeply inhaled the crisp air. Closing her eyes, she slowly exhaled.

"Are you going into a trance, or something?" Ryan asked.

"Not really," Alexa replied, opening her eyes. "Just trying to let go of my stress, clear my mind, and listen to nature."

Alexa walked to a grassy, shaded area, crossed her long legs at the ankles, and with the grace of a gazelle, lowered herself to the ground. Sitting cross-legged, she tilted her head upwards, squinting against the sun peaking through the leaves of the massive oak.

"Sit," she said, patting the ground next to her.

"What? No 'please'? You know, I don't roll over and play dead either." Crinkles in the corners of Ryan's eyes betrayed his somber tone.

"Okay then. Please sit. I have something I want to talk to you about, and don't want to get a stiff neck doing it."

Ryan mimicked Alexa's maneuver to the ground, sitting cross-legged next to her.

"Wow, you're rather limber for a guy," Alexa said, smiling.

"Yoga."

"You take yoga? I'm impressed. So, you understand about getting in touch with nature."

"Hey, I only do it to keep in shape," Ryan said. "Don't start thinking I'm a guy who's in touch with his sensitive side." He scowled to make his point. "Now, what was it you wanted to discuss?"

Alexa pulled her knees up to her chest, wrapping her arms around them, resting her chin on her knees.

"I don't know whether I'm cut out for law enforcement," she said, staring straight ahead at the river.

"What makes you think that? In my book, you're doing a great job."

"I get the intellectual part of everything, but I just can't get my head around what makes criminals do what they do."

"It's simple. They're sick freaks," Ryan said, shrugging.

"That's way over-simplifying it, don't you think? I mean, look at nature. Sure, you have predators and victims. But their incentive is survival ... or protection. I get that the human brain is more complex, and the free will thing, and all. But what I don't understand is what motivates someone to intentionally look at another human being in the face, and then kill him ... or her. What's going on in their heads?" Alexa turned her face to Ryan, eyebrows drawn together.

"You're searching for human motivation that conflicts with your morals. You can study it in school, and it comes down to the evils we abhor as a civilized people – greed, jealousy, anger, and the like. And don't forget money as an incentive. With some crimes, drugs alter behaviors to make people do the unthinkable."

"I get that part," Alexa said. "I took a class in criminal behavior. I just can't think like a criminal. You know, really understand where they come from."

"Don't try. As law enforcement officers, it's not our job to change who we are to become them. Believe me, you don't want to let your brain go there. We study criminal behavior to catch the freaks and bring them down. Remember our code – to protect and serve. Who are we protecting and serving? Certainly not the bad guys. We're doing it for the good guys."

Ryan ran his hand down Alexa's arm, and then grasped her hands.

"You'll be great in this field. You care, and you're smart. That's what's important."

Alexa dropped her arms from around her legs, raising to her feet as easily as she had sat down. Ryan pushed himself up with his hands.

"You've got some stuff on your butt," he said, gently wiping her pants before doing the same to his own.

"Thanks," Alexa said. "Not for the butt wiping, but for listening."

Ryan guided Alexa under the tree. His right hand caressed her face, and then tilted her chin up to meet his face. He pulled her to him, left hand in the small of her back.

Gasping slightly, Alexa's mouth met his. They kissed tenderly.

"Umm," Alexa whispered, stepping away, "we better keep walking. Don't want to start something we can't finish."

"Who says we can't finish?" Ryan asked, pulling her back to him.

"But it's broad daylight. And you're a cop. Besides which, you're clogging my head rather than clearing it." Releasing the twitter rolling inside her body, Alexa's head tilted back as she burst out laughing.

"Okay then, let's just continue our stroll," Ryan chuckled.

Walking under the Longfellow Bridge, Alexa's shoulders heaved, quivering. She crossed her arms, rubbing her biceps, as they continued walking.

"You okay?" Ryan asked.

"Just got a weird feeling." She stopped, gazing at the river. "Isn't this where Julia's body was found?"

"Yes, it is," Ryan murmured. "You're not getting a vision, or something, are you?"

"No," Alexa said, flatly.

Sensing she needed to be alone for awhile, Ryan strolled to a nearby bench, and sat, continuing to stare at her.

Alexa inhaled, filling her lungs with summer's breath. Slowly exhaling, she stared at the murky river. Gentle ripples moved in the direction of the outgoing tide. A breeze stirred, whipping a strand of hair across her forehead. She reached up, and then tucked her hair behind her ears.

"Come on, you old river," she whispered, "give up your secrets."

She heard the mournful wail of a siren in the background. Closing her eyes, she recalled her mother's dream. The woman – Julia – floating. The three men holding a red scarf. The mysterious, looming figure. Opening her eyes, she noticed a darkened area ripple from the abutment toward the river's edge. She blinked, and then refocused on the area. It disappeared.

A shadow crossed Alexa's. Slowly, she turned, heart skipping. A teenage boy stood near her, arms cradling a dozen roses tied with a red ribbon. He looked harmless. In fact, he reminded her of Johnny.

"You okay?" the stranger asked.

"Yes, I'm fine." Alexa stared at the flowers. "Are those for someone special?" she asked.

"Yeah." The stranger grinned. "My girlfriend. We're celebrating our three-month anniversary."

Ryan sauntered to Alexa's side, possessively … protectively … putting his arm around her shoulders. The young man grinned.

"Okay, then," he said, waving as he walked away. "Have a good day."

Alexa and Ryan watched the young man as he disappeared into the shadows under the bridge. Alexa's gaze returned to the river. She smiled, nodding.

"We need to have a talk with Rosie," Alexa said.

CHAPTER 41

"So, tell all," Kate said, helping Alexa clear the dinner table. "What'd Eddie say?"

"Well, Frank persuaded him to be honest with us," Alexa responded, carrying an armful of dishes into the kitchen.

"He break out the rubber hose, or brass knuckles?" Kate's eyes twinkled with mirth.

"Oh, Nana Kate, you are such a hoot. You know you can't bait me like mom."

"Yeah, that's right. But you can't blame me for trying." Kate shrugged.

"Anyway," Alexa started, while rinsing and stacking the dishes in the washer, "Eddie admitted he saw someone else in Nick's apartment that night."

"So, who was it?" Lilith asked, entering the kitchen.

"Rosie." Kate and Lilith exchanged a glance.

"What the hell was she doing there?" Kate asked.

"Not sure. We all know the apartment was supposed to have been Nick's secret rendezvous place. And there's something more curious." Alexa paused turning to face Lilith and Kate. Lilith moved over to the sink to continue loading the dishwasher. "Rosie was holding lingerie when Eddie saw her. Nick pretended, or at least implied, they belonged to Rosie. But I suspect they may have been Julia's missing undergarments."

"Holy jamoly," Lilith exclaimed. "So the lingerie would tie Julia into at least having visited Nick's apartment that night."

"That's right," Alexa said. "But it still doesn't tell us what happened. Was she there when Rosie arrived? Or did she leave before Rosie got there? And if she left, where'd she go?"

"Well, you can bet Nick and Julia had sex," Kate stated confidently, nodding her head for emphasis.

"Now how can you be so positive about that?" Lilith asked.

"How else would Rosie have her hands on Julia's undies?"

"We still don't know for sure they were Julia's," Alexa said. "And chances are we never will. I'm just going on a theory they were Julia's." Alexa looked down, shaking her head, before continuing. "So much of this case is based on the theoretical. If it wasn't such an old case, we'd have more hard facts. A bit discouraging."

"Oh, honey," Kate said, wrapping an arm around Alexa's waist, "you're finding out more than the cops did back then. Don't give up. The answers will come out. You'll see."

Alexa sighed, looking directly at Kate and Lilith.

"I did come up with another possibility, involving Greg Lyons." Alexa described her theory to them. Both agreed it held promise.

"So, what's your next step?" Lilith asked.

"Ryan and Frank are poking around about bars in the old neighborhood to see if any of Greg Lyons' old pals still frequent them. Since I insisted on being in on all interviews, we're planning to go out Friday night."

"You finally have a date with Ryan?" Kate asked, eyes gleaming mischievously.

"Frank's going with us."

"I'm not comfortable with you going into skuzzy bars," Lilith protested. "Dangerous sorts hang out in them."

"Oh, for Pete's sake, Mom. I'm going with two armed cops."

"Can I go, too?" Kate asked, turning her doe-eyes to Alexa.

"What?" Lilith asked.

"I wanna go. Like a double date."

"I don't know, Nana Kate," Alexa said, stifling a chuckle.

"Hey, these guys are more my age. And we went to the same high school. I could be an asset." Kate paused, holding up two fingers. "And I promise I won't embarrass you. No dancing in a cage, or anything."

"No what?" Alexa asked.

"Dancing in a cage."

"When did you ever do that?"

"I was a go-go dancer when your Mom was little. Did it as a side job to earn a bit of money. Paid pretty well." Kate's eyes danced.

"That explains some of the clothes in your old wardrobe." Alexa paused. "Okay, then. You can come along." She released her stifled laughter.

When her laughter subsided, Alexa moved to a stool, sitting, while propping her face in her hand. Her eyebrows creased. She wasn't sure how to tell her Mom and Nana Kate about Ryan's other theory.

"After I told Ryan my theory about Greg, he posed a rather bizarre scenario of his own on Julia's death," Alexa said, feeling her cheeks redden.

"Why are you blushing?" Kate asked.

"Have you ever heard of erotic asphyxiation?" The heat in Alexa's face deepened. A plate clattered out of Lilith's hands into the sink.

"What the hell is that guy telling you?" Lilith asked, annoyance edging her voice.

"Now don't get yourself in a twitter," Kate said, trying to calm her own heart's pounding. "I'm sure there's a reasonable explanation." She stared doe-eyed at Alexa.

"Well, Ryan said maybe the strangulation was an accident that happened while Julia and Nick were having sex," Alexa explained. "But it still doesn't explain what Rosie was doing there." She stroked her chin before continuing. "Unless, Eddie was lying again, and it wasn't Rosie in the apartment." She shook her head. "But Frank would have flushed out the lie. And Eddie's body language didn't contradict his story." Alexa sighed in frustration.

"I do have one more interview idea," Alexa said, looking from Kate to Lilith. "There's only one person still alive who may be able to fill in the blanks. But I'm not sure about how to go about setting up a meeting."

"Who is it?" Lilith asked. "Maybe we can help."

"I was hoping you'd say that. We need to talk to Rosie. According to Eddie, she's in some assisted living place in Quincy."

"I'm still in contact with her granddaughter from time to time," Lilith said. "I'll give Kathy a call to see what we can set up."

Kate wandered around the kitchen, pretending to check the counters for dust. Slowly, she turned to Lilith and Alexa, raising her arm.

"I know just how to stage the interview," Kate announced. Lilith and Alexa rolled their eyes.

Later that evening, Lilith called Kathy. After the usual pleasantries about their families, Lilith explained the purpose of her call.

"Alexa's interning at the police department this summer, and is working on a cold case for credit. The case has special significance to our family." Lilith cleared her throat. "She's looking into the death of my grandmother, Julia O'Shea."

"What's that got to do with Grandma?" Kathy asked.

"As it turns out, your grandmother may have been one of the last people to see Julia alive." Lilith avoided giving Kathy all the sordid details.

"I knew there was some history between them, but I always thought they weren't on speaking terms. Did they reconcile, or something?"

"I'm not sure," Lilith said. "And our information may not be accurate. But if your grandmother can help us out, we'd really appreciate it. Frankly," she continued in a conspiratorial tone, "we've reached a wall. She could be instrumental in helping us solve this mystery."

"You know, she's rather old, and her mind isn't what it once was," Kathy said, chuckling. "Not that she ever had a great mind."

CHAPTER 42

Alexa and Kate dressed in jeans and tee shirts for their Friday night "date" with Frank and Ryan. Spending the past couple of days asking around, Frank and Ryan had zeroed in on the bar frequented by Greg Lyons' old drinking pals.

"Everything looks so different," Kate sighed as they drove into the neighborhood of her youth. "Trees are larger. Houses in disrepair. Some have been replaced with apartment buildings. Such a shame."

Parallel parking her car on a side street, Alexa checked her makeup in the visor mirror. Normally, she wore little makeup, but tonight, she'd applied eye shadow, extra mascara, blush, and red lipstick. Her long, blonde hair hung loose. She felt a bit trampy, but decided her look would fit the scene of the bar. She glanced at Kate, pleased. Going for an appearance to match their surroundings, Kate's shirt disguised her shapely figure, while her over-done makeup and unkempt hairstyle reflected a woman who had seen the inside of too many bars.

"Let's go," Frank announced, opening the door. "Ladies first."

They entered the barely-lit smoke-filled room. Apparently, the owner gave no heed to smoking restrictions in public spaces. A long bar, scarred with rings from years of spilled drinks, ran along the right side of the establishment. Neon beer signs blinked a Morse code behind the bar, back-lighting rows of liquor bottles. Round wooden tables and chairs, dented and slashed by boisterous patrons, occupied half the room. In the back corner, three pool tables were illuminated by lights shaded with dust and grime-covered fake Tiffany octagons. A juke box blared tunes from the seventies.

The clientele ranged in age from forties to eighties – none particularly attractive. The men were mostly attired in well-worn jeans, with shirts alternately drooping on skeletal frames or stretched snugly across stomachs enlarged by years of imbibing drink and bar food. The age of the women was indistinguishable;

their faces thickly powdered over mottled wrinkles, and bleary eyes edged in black liner. Most patrons sat on the dozen or so bar stools, supporting themselves along the wooden rail. Several men gathered around the pool tables. All tables were vacant.

Seeing no barstools available, Ryan guided Alexa and Kate to a table near the pool tables. Conversations stopped and heads turned as they weaved around the tables. Frank sauntered behind them, covertly eyeing the patrons.

"I don't think they have a waitress," Kate yelled to Ryan over the music. "Guess our best bet is to drink beer. I'll have anything in a bottle. No mug. I'll be a bottle baby tonight."

Ryan headed to the bar to order three beers, and a soft drink for Alexa. Most eyes stayed on Kate, Alexa and Frank. Several women watched Ryan, admiringly. Through beer-soaked brains they imagined the possibilities of seducing a new, handsome young man.

"Not from around here, are ya?" the bartender asked as he handed Ryan four bottles. Patrons on nearby barstools turned to hear his answer.

"My date's grandmother grew up here," Ryan answered, following a pre-arranged script. "She's in town visiting, and wanted to take a look at the old neighborhood. See if any of her old classmates were still around."

"What's her name?" a patron slurred. A large man, stomach swelled from years of swilling beer, his watery eyes told of hours already spent propped on his barstool.

"Kate Gallagher."

"Where'd she live?" the patron pressed.

"Don't really know," Ryan said, shrugging.

"Maybe I'll come over and ask her. Be a regular welcoming committee." The large man snickered as he clumsily turned on his stool. Holding onto the bar for support, he gingerly placed his feet on the floor.

Ryan carried the beverages back to the table. The man staggered to the pool tables.

"Hey, Bobby, Lefty" the man yelled to two elderly patrons, "got a visitor here from the old days. 'Member anyone named Kate Gallagher?" He pointed at Kate. The two men leaned forward on their pool cues, staring.

"Hard to tell," one of them replied. "Eyes ain't what they useta be."

"Neither are your other parts," the other man guffawed. The first man punched his buddy in the shoulder.

"Well, it looks like I'm just going to have to take control of things here," Kate said, rising from her chair.

"Nana Kate, where are you going?"

"This could take all night if I don't get things started. And I don't want to miss my late-night shows." Before anyone could stop her, Kate left their table, headed for the pool tables. Frank followed her.

"Hey fellas," Kate said, extending her hand, "I'm Kate Gallagher. I grew up over on Meadow Street. Grey house with blue shutters. I live down in Florida now. Just came up to visit my daughter and her kids. Thought it would be fun to hang around the old neighborhood for the night." She paused. The three men stared silently. "I know it's been years, but do I know any of you? What are your names?"

"Who's he?" the large man asked, head motioning to Frank.

"I think he's supposed to be a fix-up," Kate said, leaning into the large man. "He's my granddaughter's boyfriend's uncle. Name's Frank." The large man smiled.

"I'm Davey Jones," the large man said, shaking Kate's hand. "Nicknamed Locker."

"I can see why, for several reasons," Kate chuckled. He snickered in return.

"This here's Lefty Watson, and that's Bobby Nichols." Both men nodded.

"Bobby Nichols," Kate said, hesitantly. "I think we went to high school together. Did you marry Missy Jamison?"

"Yeah."

"Why he's down here every night," Lefty said, laughing.

"Why don't you guys join us?" Kate said. "Let me buy you a round. My granddaughter might enjoy hearing stories from the old days."

The men followed Kate to the table, pulling up chairs as Ryan and Alexa shifted their chairs to make room. Kate introduced everyone before sending Ryan to the bar for more drinks.

"Hey, sweet cheeks," a forty-something woman at the bar shouted to Ryan. "Looks like your table got a bit crowded. Too many men. Wanna join a real woman for a drink? Might lead someplace nice." She smiled, showing uneven, yellowed teeth in her bloated face.

"Put a sock in it, Annie," the bartender bellowed. "Ain't your kind." She turned back to the glass in front of her. Ryan placed an extra ten dollars on the bar before heading back to the table.

"Now I remember you," Bobby said. "Dated Jack O'Shea, didn't ya?"

"Yes, I did."

"Heard he got killed in Nam. What a shame. Good guy. Helluva football player. Got us to the regionals junior year. Coulda gone higher senior year if he hadn't got … um … sick."

"That the guy who's mother got killed your senior year?" Lefty asked. "Found her in the Charles, right?"

"Yeah." Bobby lowered his head, shaking it from side to side. He grinned crookedly as he looked up. "Dated his younger sister, Colleen, before Missy got her claws in me. Shoulda stayed with her. But I let my lower brain do the thinking back then. And look where it got me."

"Yeah, hanging out with the likes of us," Locker said. The three men exchanged shoulder punches, laughing.

"You guys remember old man Lyons?" Kate asked. "Used to have a lot of parties at his house?"

"Yeah. Weird guy," Lefty said. "Always wanted to hang around with his kid's friends. Harmless enough. Wasn't no pedophile or nothing. Just liked to party." He stared intently at Kate before continuing, "Bit of a lech, he was. Hit on anything in a skirt. Always hanging all over Missy's Mom, Rosie. But I think she liked it. He come on to you or something?"

"Oh goodness, no," Kate said. "But Jack told me Greg used to get fresh with Mrs. O'Shea. In fact, she barred him from their house. Whatever happened to him?"

"Oh, he died years ago," Bobby said. "Drink got to him. We useta call him the Mayor. He'd go bar hopping with us in our younger days. Picked up the tab a lot, so we let him think he was part of the gang. Took us to some high-class places every now and then."

190

"Like where?" Kate asked, turning her doe-eyed stare to the men.

"Went to someplace on Beacon Hill once," Lefty said, looking at his friends. "Remember the times he took us to The Club?"

"Yeah," Locker said. "Real classy joint. Had some fag piano player. But he was good. Got everyone singing." He paused as a distant memory plowed its way through his brain, mushy from too many years of over-imbibing. "You guys remember the night we saw Mrs. O'Shea in there singing? Great voice. And what a looker."

"That the night the Mayor got kicked out?" Lefty asked, chuckling.

"Yeah. We hadta go after him 'cause he drove."

"So, you all left together?" Kate asked, glancing at Alexa and Ryan.

"Yeah. He was stumbling half-way down the block when we caught up to him. That was one scary drive home. Good thing there wasn't much traffic." Locker paused again. "Funny thing. After he dropped us off at my house, I remember seeing him pull into the O'Shea's driveway. Figured he was so drunk he forgot where he lived. So I ran up the street after him. Saw him ring the doorbell. Old man O'Shea answered. Had some loud words, then O'Shea pushed Greg out and slammed the door. Greg stumbled to his car, got in, and took off. Saw his brake lights as he turned the corner to his house."

"So you figure he went home?"

"Wanted to make sure he was okay, so I ran to the corner. Saw him pull into his own driveway." Locker chuckled. "Stumbled outta his car, stopped in the middle of his lawn, bent over and puked all over his wife's flowers. Bet she was pissed." Locker shook his head. "Helluva night that was. Hard to forget."

"Well, fellas," Kate said. "It's been fun catching up. But it's getting to my witching hour."

"Aww," Bobby groaned, "can't ya stay a bit longer? One more drink."

"I'd love to, but I promised my daughter I'd be home by eleven. I don't want to worry her."

"On a curfew, huh?" Lefty said, grinning lopsidedly.

"Well, yes. But it's better than hearing her lecture me in the morning." Kate smiled and turned to Ryan. "Be a dear, and get these guys one more round, would you? It'll be my parting gift to them."

After Ryan returned with the drinks, Kate hugged each of the men. Ryan, Frank and Alexa shook their hands.

"Well, that was fun," Kate said when they returned to the car.

"You're one hell of an interviewer," Frank said.

"I'm just good with drunks."

"I guess that blows my theory about Greg Lyons killing Julia," Alexa sighed.

"Don't worry, dear," Kate said, patting Alexa's hand. "As Scarlett O'Hara said, 'Tomorrow is another day.' Maybe we'll find out more when we talk to Rosie."

CHAPTER **43**

The following week, the entire crew headed south on I-93 to Quincy. Alexa and Ryan rode in one car, while Frank chauffeured Kate, Lilith and Johnny. Kate had insisted Johnny join them to complete her plan.

"Okay, everyone," Frank announced during the drive, "time for a local history lesson." The wipers squeaked across the windshield, battling a heavy downpour. "Which came first? The town of Quincy, or the president John Quincy Adams?"

"The town," Johnny stated firmly. "It was named for the president's great grandfather, Colonel John Quincy, who was Abigail Adams's grandfather. Learned that in fourth grade history."

"Okay, so give the lad an A," Frank grunted.

Kate struggled against her seat belt looking at the sky through the windshield.

"What are you doing?" Frank asked.

"Rainbow hunting."

"You're not gonna find any rainbows in this deluge. Can't see more than a hundred yards ahead."

"I'm preparing to spot one," Kate said.

"And just how are you doing that?"

"I'm getting a fix on where the sun is. See? You can barely see it peeking through right over there." Kate pointed to a small crevice in the darkened sky. "Rainbows appear in the sky opposite from the sun."

"Well, good luck on that one," Frank muttered.

The cars pulled into the parking lot of a large, colonial home, built in the early nineteen-hundreds. Once occupied by people of wealth, it was renovated into its current configuration of a nursing home in the nineteen-eighties. A well-manicured lawn formed the carpet for beds of roses, daisies and daylilies. Empty rocking chairs lined the front porch that disappeared around the sides of the home.

Rosie's granddaughter, Kathy, met them at the front door. Shaking her umbrella before placing it in a stand inside the foyer, Lilith introduced her family, then Frank and Ryan.

"What a nice dress," Kathy said, eyeing Lilith as they walked into the home. "Is it coming back in style?"

"You know I always liked dressing up," Lilith giggled. "Maybe I can be ahead of a fashion statement, rather than following one ... for a change."

The previous night, Kate insisted Lilith and Alexa accompany her to the attic. Rummaging through her old wardrobe, Kate pulled out a flowered dress. At Kate's urging, Lilith gingerly slipped the dress over her head. It fit perfectly, except for being shorter on Lilith than when Kate had worn it years before. Kate pulled a scarf from a box buried in the bottom of the wardrobe, and wrapped it loosely around Lilith's neck. Kate nodded and smiled at the result. Lilith looked exactly like Julia.

"So were you all planning to go into grandma's room?" Kathy asked, looking at the group. "It's not very large, and there's limited seating."

"We'll start out with having Ryan, Lilith, Alexa and Johnny go in for a visit," Kate replied. Frank shuffled his feet, moving forward slightly. Kate glared at him, imperceptibly shaking her head. This was her plan. Turning back to Kathy, she continued, "If you don't mind, Frank and I will hover by the door." Kathy shrugged her agreement.

Rosie resided on the second floor, occupied by residents with limited mobility. Meals were delivered to their rooms. Two former bedrooms on the floor had been converted into a general entertainment area, equipped with a television and several game tables. Rosie's twenty-by-twenty-foot room was decorated in a flower motif, predominantly pink roses. Her bed, window, table and chairs were in full bloom with shades of pink.

Rosie appeared to be expecting company. She lay at a forty-five degree angle atop the bedspread's roses, propped up by overstuffed pillows. She was dressed in a pink robe, with matching slippers. Ruffles around her collar and sleeves accentuated, rather than disguised, her weathered skin. Her gray, brittle hair was smoothed away from her face – several wiry sprigs escaped randomly around her head. Face over-powdered and lips smeared with bright red coloring added to the overall appearance of an aging clown.

Kathy escorted her guests to the far side of Rosie's bed. Rosie's rheumy eyes followed them, squinting against the light filtering through the shear curtains.

"Grandma," Kathy whispered, leaning into Rosie, "you have some visitors."

"Well, step aside, child, so I can see them," Rosie rasped.

As planned, Lilith and Johnny stepped forward. Ryan and Alexa sat in chairs by the window.

"This is," Kathy started, turning sideways to allow Lilith and Johnny room next to the bed.

With a sharp snap of her hand, Rosie silenced Kathy. Rosie struggled against the pillows, leaning forward. The red smear broadened.

"So you've come to visit me, have you?" Rosie asked, looking from Lilith to Johnny. "And I see you've brought Jack. Handsome boy, he is. Did I ever tell you that? Where's that Missy? They make such a cute couple. She should be here." Rosie turned her head back and forth. "Missy. Missy," she yelled. "Damned kid is never where she should be. Oh well. I'll have her bring us some tea once she gets home."

Johnny looked at his mother, confused by this old woman's rambling. Lilith glanced at him, slowly shaking her head. Kate's plan was working.

CHAPTER 44

R osie struggled to remain upright. Eyes narrowed, she looked at Lilith, arm extended, arthritic finger pointing.

"You think I'm just a stupid, flighty, blonde bimbo," Rosie croaked. "All of you think that." She lowered her arm, then pointed to her forehead. "But I got smarts you don't know about." She cackled as she lowered herself to rest on the pillows. She folded her hands across her stomach and slowly closed her eyes, smiling.

"Is she okay?" Lilith whispered to Kathy.

"Yeah. That's how she always looks when her mind regresses. She'll come out of it in a few minutes."

Rosie's mind wandered back to a time more than half a century earlier.

From the first time I saw Nick, I knew I had to have him. Didn't care he was dating Julia. I knew she'd get bored with him in time. He wasn't really her type. She liked them tall and slim, but muscular … and faithful. Nick wasn't any of those. He was a big man. Tall, broad-shouldered, thick chest. And didn't have a faithful bone in his body. Fine with me. He just needed a woman who tolerated his weaknesses. And he was smart. Knew a good deal when he saw it. So I found a guy for Julia, then swooped in on Nick. Never knew what hit them.

Try as I did, I couldn't get pregnant by Nick. That was my plan. We screwed everywhere and in every way. So, I had to change my plan a bit. Found some guy who looked kinda like Nick, and screwed him. Greg Lyons was his name. Handsome enough when he was young. Aged ugly. My plan worked. Told Nick the kid was his. Dumb shit never knew any different. Once he married me, I knew I'd never let him go.

The deal between Nick and me was I'd turn a blind eye to his cavorting, and keep a good house for him. In return, he let me buy whatever I wanted. He made a real good living, so I did a lot of buying. Now and then, he'd scratch my itch. He sure knew how to work it. But then, so did I.

I always knew he took his whores someplace. Didn't know where. Didn't really care. But that old curious cat got hold of me when I found the key in his jacket pocket. Didn't mean to. Just checking the pockets before sending his suits to the cleaners. But there it was. Even had a label with the address on it. What a dumb shit. So I took the key and had a copy made, then slipped it back in the pocket. Next time I checked, it was gone. Probably thought I was too stupid to find it, or know what it was.

One day shopping on Newbury Street, I decided to check out his girlie pad, so I headed over to Marlborough. It was on the second floor. Just a one bedroom place. Not much furniture. A few knick-knacks about. Satisfied he didn't spend much on furnishing the place, I left. Didn't leave any sign I'd been there.

Then Julia came back in the picture.

Having lunch a couple of months later, ready for more shopping, I spotted them. They were strolling down the street hand-in-hand, looking like some love-struck couple … laughing. My stomach burned. Were they laughing at me? About how stupid I was? I watched as they headed in the direction of his apartment. The world turned red. Everything I looked at had a scarlet tint. My temples pounded. Started following them. But then what? What would I say … or do … if I caught up with them? I needed a plan. Had to think this one over. So I went home.

Nick stayed out the next two nights. I knew he was with her. Screwing her. Probably buying her pretty things. My money. How dare he spend it on her. Our deal was, it was all mine. I let him have his fun. But now he'd broken our deal. I couldn't … no, wouldn't … let him get away with it. I'd show him who was smart, and who was stupid.

CHAPTER 45

R osie's eyes fluttered, then opened wide. Slowly, her head turned toward Lilith.

"Whore," Rosie spat. Then, her eyes closed as her head returned to its resting position.

"I don't care what kind of crazy old bat she is," Johnny said, voice straining with anger. "No one talks to my mother that way."

"Calm down, honey," Lilith said, putting her hand on his arm. "She still thinks I'm Julia. Let her go. I think we're almost there."

Johnny sighed, walking toward the window. He stared out, trying to release his anger. Alexa went to him, wrapping her arm around his shoulder. He leaned into her.

"It's okay," Alexa cooed. "We have to trust Mom knows what she's doing."

Rosie drifted back to the past.

The third day Nick didn't show up, I went to Marlborough Street. I waited 'til I saw them come out of the building. Followed them. They went to some ritzy joint around the corner, named The Club. I didn't go in. Could hear the music when the door opened. Waited around a bit, to make sure they were staying for awhile. Then I headed back to the apartment.

Time passed so slowly. Could hear the damn clock ticking off the minutes. God, it was annoying. I knew silence would be worse. Thought about turning on the radio or TV. But I wanted to surprise them. Couldn't make any noise. So, I just sat there, with one lamp on.

I heard them laughing. Echoed in the stairwell and hall. Mocking me. I turned off the light, and sat in the corner. The key turned in the lock. The knob creaked when he turned it. A dim light entered the apartment, then left as the door closed. He turned on a small lamp next to the door.

Nick grabbed Julia to him, kissing her so passionately. She moaned. He led her into the bedroom. They never even noticed I was

199

there. I felt small … like an intruder. But I wasn't, dammit. He was my man, not hers. She'd had her chance and thrown him away. Who the hell did she think she was? He wasn't some plaything for her pleasure. He … was … mine.

I heard them. The bed squeaked under them. Could hear their panting … groans. My hands opened and closed into fists. Then opened again around something. Felt like a head. I squeezed my hands around it, choking it.

Walking into the bedroom, I saw him on top of her. He was in her. Their bodies moved in perfect rhythm. They didn't know I was there.

I lifted the head-thing in my hands, and brought it down on Nick. His body collapsed on top of her. I heard a whooshing sound come from her. She was trapped under his weight. Her one free arm flailed against him, trying to push him off. But he was out cold. Blood trickled from his head. It was time.

The head-thing in my hands thudded as it hit the floor. I walked to where she could see me. Those eyes. The eyes that captivated everyone stared at me, pleading. I laughed, just as they had laughed at me. Those eyes had no effect on me.

I noticed the scarf around her neck. That long, white, perfect neck. The one he had probably nibbled hundreds of times. I grabbed the ends of the scarf. Pulling her hair, I lifted her head, and wrapped the scarf around her neck, alternating one end, then the other. I let her head drop. I grabbed the scarf, looped the ends in my hands several times so it wouldn't slip. Then I pulled hard as I could. She tried to cough with the little air left in her lungs. Her hand clawed at my arm. I released the scarf just long enough to kneel on her free arm. I pulled until she stopped struggling. Her tongue stuck out of her mouth at an odd angle. Her eyes bulged.

Nick stirred. He groaned. Slowly, he rolled off Julia's dead body. I had rescued him from her.

I ran to the kitchen to get some ice. Maybe he needed a drink, too. I struggled with the ice tray. Stupid metal contraption. Finally freeing the ice, I wrapped cubes in a towel, saving some for that drink. I heard Nick scream – a low, mournful wail. I ran back to him.

"It's okay, baby," I whispered, gently placing the towel on his head. "I'm here for you, like always." His face was contorted with pain. Tears streamed down his cheeks. He looked up at me, staring … just staring. Like I was a stranger, or something.

"What have you done?" he asked. His eyes accused me, but I wasn't the villain. He had to see that.

"Freed you from her spell is what I've done," I told him.

"My god, Rosie, she's dead. You killed her."

He stood up, wobbled, then sat back down on the bed. He grabbed the towel from my hand. He lowered his head, putting the towel back on it. The bleeding had stopped.

I just stood there. Didn't know what to say or do. I had done my part. He needed to take over. I waited for his commands. I didn't expect what came next.

Nick slowly stood, barely wobbling this time. He dropped the towel on the bed, and walked over to me. His eyes were dull. Like he was looking at me, but not seeing me. He needed ... no, I needed ... his arms around me. He raised his hand. Before I could blink, I felt the sting on my cheek. Tasted blood. I collapsed to the floor. He grabbed my arms, lifting me up. My head thrashed back and forth. I felt like a rag doll. My shoulders hurt where he squeezed them. He yelled at me, but I couldn't understand what he was saying.

Finally, it stopped. He pushed me away, and walked into the bathroom, closing the door. I heard water running, then turn off. The door opened. His hair was wet, face dried of its tears. He grabbed the towel before heading into the kitchen. I ran after him. He pulled one glass from a cabinet, filled it with the remaining ice, grabbed a whiskey bottle off the counter, and poured the amber liquid over the ice. He gulped the drink, then poured another, and downed it. I waited. Setting the glass on the counter, he turned to me.

"Well, you stupid bitch," he said, "you've really done it this time. And I'll have to clean up your mess, 'cause you're too stupid to know what to do." He smirked. I couldn't believe he was mocking me. I had saved him. Coulda killed him, too. But I didn't. I knew once her spell was broken, he'd wanna be with me. Why was he being like this? But then, a big part of me wanted him to take control. That's what he was doing. He was now saving me, because he loved me. Yes. After everything, he really loved me. So, I'd do whatever he wanted.

CHAPTER 46

"**E**verybody back in position," Lilith commanded. "She's coming around." Everyone had gathered around the bed, listening. Rosie's musings had not been silent.

Back in their original places, they watched as Rosie's eyes crept open. Her focus remained on Lilith.

"He did love me, after all," she whispered. Rosie blinked several times, suddenly sitting upright. Her mouth opened, and a high-pitched scream escaped.

"No, no, no," she yelled. "It can't be you. You're dead. I saw … I did … can't be."

Rosie closed her eyes, and shook her head back and forth several times. She moaned as she collapsed back on the pillows.

A minute later, her eyes opened, clearer than before. They drifted around the room, surveying each of her visitors.

"Who the hell are you people?" Rosie asked. She looked at Kathy. "Well, of course I know you, dear. How's my favorite granddaughter?"

"I'm fine, Grandma," Kathy responded gently, her voice disguising the shock of everything she'd heard. "I'll let your other visitors introduce themselves." Kathy turned to Lilith.

"Hi, Mrs. Jamison," Lilith said. "I'm an old friend of Kathy's, Lilly."

"Oh, I remember you now," Rosie said, blinking. "You used to come by the house. Was a cheerleader with Kathy. But that was years ago."

"Yes, ma'am, it was. These are my children, Johnny and Alexa." Lilith motioned for them to step forward. Rosie nodded.

Not waiting for Lilith's introduction, Kate moved to the side of the bed, directly in front of Rosie.

"Don't know if you remember me, or not," Kate said without emotion. "I'm Kate Gallagher. Lilith's my daughter. Mine and Jack O'Shea's."

Rosie's eyes narrowed, lips pursed. She stared, unblinking, at Kate.

"Never liked you," Rosie sneered. "Thought you were so much better than my Missy." She cackled. "What, you get knocked up by Jack?" Rosie's features hardened as she continued talking. "Thought he died in Nam. Served him right, the way he treated my Missy. He was no better than his mom. Always felt sorry for his dad. Hard-working man, he was. Didn't deserve to have that bitch as a wife. Her whoring around on him all the time. Crazy as a loon, too. Jack took after her ... plum crazy. Your daughter inherit that?"

Kate felt a heat-wave rumble from her stomach to her head. She wanted to slap the wickedness from Rosie, but refrained.

"So, what're you doing here?" Rosie spat.

"We came to find out who killed Jack's mother," Kate said, flatly.

"And you think I'd tell you anything?" Rosie cackled.

"You already have, you stupid old bat. The gig's up. Didn't know you talked in your sleep, did you?" Kate smiled. "All we need to know is how she got to the river."

The powder on Rosie's face grayed. Her clown mouth opened, sucking in air. Her hands groped her neck, eyes bulged.

"Oh no you don't," Kate hissed, leaning closer to Rosie. "You're not getting off that easy. Death will not rescue you ... yet. Now talk."

Rosie's hands dropped back to her chest. The red smear turned up. Her eyes sparkled with evil. She pushed herself upright, still leaning into the pillows.

"What the hell," Rosie said, waving her hand dismissively. "I'm old. Can't hurt to brag a bit about how clever my Nick was. It was him who figured out the river would erase any evidence. Wouldn't let me touch her anymore. He put her dress back on, so's she'd look decent. He handled his dumb-ass nephew cop when he came to the door. Yelled at me for almost blowing it. But my Nick was clever. Always thought on his feet. Nick and me waited 'til the wee hours to leave. Wanted to make sure nobody was around. He carried her down the steps and to his car. Told me to just go home. I offered to clean up the apartment. But he said no, for me to just leave." Rosie paused, looking at Kathy.

"I see you're wearing those earrings I gave you," she said. Kathy raised her hand to her ear, gently stoking the dangling jewelry – blue stones surrounded by diamonds.

"Nick bought 'em," Rosie said. "But not for me. She had 'em on that night. Shoulda been mine. So, I took 'em. Nick never knew." Looking back at Kate, Rosie continued.

"Nick didn't come home 'til the next night. Asked him what he'd done with her. He just looked at me, real sad-like, and told me it wasn't none of my business, he'd taken care of it. Guess he'd done as he said he would – thrown her in the river." Rosie paused, clearing her throat, then cackled. "Almost wish she hadn't been quite dead, so's she'd drown, too."

"My God," Kate said, backing away from the bed, "you are a horrid creature, aren't you? How could Nick continue living with the likes of you?"

Rosie's smile faded. The crevices around her mouth and eyes deepened.

"He never touched me again after that night," she whispered. A tear coursed down her cheek as she slumped into her pillows and closed her eyes.

Leaving the room, Kathy removed the earrings, and handed them to Lilith.

Outside, the rain had subsided, turning into a gentle mist.

"Look, Nana Kate," Johnny said, pointing to the sky. "There's your rainbow."

"Oh honey, it's magnificent."

"It's a double one, Nana."

Kate turned from the rainbows toward the sun, first squinting, and then smiling.

"Look over here, Johnny. You can barely see another one. Combined, they form a triple rainbow – a rare sight."

Everyone stood in the parking lot, alternately gazing from the brilliant double rainbow to the faint singleton in the opposite sky.

"Guess it's our lucky day," Alexa whispered.

CHAPTER 47

"**N**ow who the heck can that be, calling at suppertime?" Lilith asked the following evening, her family gathered around the dining table. She scooted her chair from the table, and walked to the kitchen to answer the phone. A minute later, she returned to the table.

"Well, who was it?" Kate asked.

"Frank. He wanted to let us know Rosie passed away in her sleep last night. I guess we should notify Mary and Colleen ... and Tony. They'd want to know everything."

"So much for putting the old bitch in shackles," Kate said. Alexa and Johnny giggled.

"Kate," Lilith said, raising her voice, "you shouldn't speak ill of the dead."

"Why the hell not? She was the devil's mistress. Good riddance to bad rubbish, I say."

"Well, maybe another adage would be truer. Maybe confession is good for the soul. Maybe she made her peace."

"And maybe pigs fly," Kate mumbled.

"Oh, I almost forgot to tell you guys," Lilith said, changing the subject. "I had bits and pieces of that dream again last night."

"Well, you already figured out most of it," Alexa said. "You know who the three men were. And my guess is the red scarf they held was a love tie to Julia. The shadowy figure must have been Rosie. The face you saw was a bust of some sort she used to thump Nick on the noggin. What's left?"

"Julia's words to me," Lilith announced. "I finally heard them." She paused to make sure everyone was listening. "She was actually singing."

"What song?" Bill asked.

"It was 'You Are My Sunshine'."

Kate's head dropped, as if her neck could no longer support it. When she looked up, tears puddled in her eyes. She sniffed quietly.

"What's the matter, Kate?" Lilith asked.

"Oh, don't mind me. I'm just getting sentimental in my old age."

"You are not old," Alexa said.

"Thank you, dear," Kate said, smiling. Her smile faded before continuing. "That's the song I sang to Jack the day his mother was buried – just before he uttered his last words to me."

"Okay, I just got the chills," Alexa said, rubbing her arms.

Kate cleared her throat and smiled.

"I'll go make those calls," she said, pushing back her chair. "Think I'll actually enjoy talking ill of the dead." Kate stopped before entering the kitchen. She turned, looking from Lilith to Alexa. "Meet me in my room in an hour. I have a surprise for you two." She chuckled as she walked to the phone.

Lilith and Alexa entered Kate's room. Music from the seventies was blaring on her CD player. The walls and furniture had an eerie glow. Everything white was blue. A lava lamp's glowing colors slowly glopped from end to end.

"Come on in," Kate beckoned. "Lock the door and take a seat." Three over-stuffed chairs were gathered in the corner. Kate sat in one.

"What's this all about?" Lilith asked. "Have you regressed into your hippie years?"

"Shush, and I'll tell you," Kate chuckled. "I figured we needed to celebrate. Three women solving a case. Three generations taking down the evil that haunted our family. No more secrets, no more lies."

Lilith noticed the champagne bottle tilted in the ice bucket on the side table. Kate grabbed the bottle by the neck, gently shaking it to remove the ice clinging to its sides. With a fluidity of motion proving her experience, she unwrapped the foil, twisted the metal coil around the cork, and then rocked the cork upward. A slight "pop" emerged as the trapped vapors escaped. Pouring the champagne into two flutes, Kate handed the glasses to Lilith and Alexa. Her glass remained on the table.

Kate reached into her shirt, dramatically pulling something from her bra.

"Is that what I think it is?" Alexa asked.

"Yep. Your mother never was good at hiding things."

Lilith's eyes widened and mouth gaped as Kate grabbed a lighter from the table, lit the joint, and then inhaled deeply. Holding her breath, she offered it to Alexa and Lilith.

"Think I'll stick with the champagne," Alexa said, shaking her head, grinning. "After all, I'm in law enforcement now. But don't worry, I won't bust you ... at least, not this time."

CPSIA information can be obtained at www.ICGtesting.com

229055LV00001B/4/P

9 781457 502675